"How about dinner? Without the kids, so we can talk."

"No. I don't do dinner."

Quinn raised an eyebrow and looked at Belle as if she'd said something ridiculous.

"What? No one ever tells you no?"

Surprise etched his brow, but then he laughed. "I was confused when you said you don't do dinner. As in, you have something against eating in the evening?"

"Oh." Her cheeks burned again. Deep in her gut she knew she would love going out with him, but then he would get to know her and… "I eat dinner, just not with people. I mean, with men." She groaned. "I don't date. I just want to be clear on the subject. I never go on dates."

"That's a shame. I think you would be a great dinner date." He grinned, and her stupid heart flipped over.

She needed to stay as far away as possible. She already had one ex-husband, and that was more than enough for her.

P. 63

A seventh-generation Texan, **Jolene Navarro** fills her life with family, faith and life's beautiful messiness. She knows that as much as the world changes, people stay the same: vow-keepers and heartbreakers. Jolene married a vow-keeper who shows her holding hands never gets old. When not writing, Jolene teaches art to inner-city teens and hangs out with her own four almost-grown kids. Find Jolene on Facebook or her blog, jolenenavarrowriter.com.

Visit the Author Profile page at Harlequin.com for more titles.

The Texan's Promise

Jolene Navarro

LOVE INSPIRED
INSPIRATIONAL ROMANCE

LOVE INSPIRED®

INSPIRATIONAL ROMANCE

Recycling programs
for this product may
not exist in your area.

ISBN-13: 978-1-335-48802-2

The Texan's Promise

Love Inspired
22 Adelaide St. West, 40th Floor
Toronto, Ontario M5H 4E3, Canada
www.Harlequin.com

Printed in U.S.A.

Every wise woman buildeth her house:
but the foolish plucketh it down with her hands.
—*Proverbs* 14:1

Jesus Alfredo Navarro

You made me laugh, wiped my tears,
cheered when I succeeded and pushed me
to live out my dreams. Thank you for being
my promise keeper and forever friend.
Oh, and doing the dishes...
especially for doing the dishes.

Chapter One

The two-year-old mare tossed her head and pawed the sand of the arena as the thunder rattled the metal roof again. The storm had rolled in fast and hard. Belle De La Rosa laid a hand on the young horse's neck. "Shhh, girl. It's okay. It's just pitter-patter on the roof."

Sometimes a little lie made everyone feel better. The goal had been to socialize the mare, but the weather had hit harder than forecasted. Now the poor baby was traumatized. The evening could end in complete disaster if the unpredictable animal panicked. She needed to get her safely back into the trailer.

"He's here." Jazmine, her brother Elijah's wife, appeared on the other side of the restless horse. Her hand was over her newly visible baby bump.

Belle closed her eyes to prevent rolling them. The De La Rosa women had joined forces in the "Find Belle a Man" campaign. The latest victim was a single dad. Selena, her cousin Xavier's wife, had met him in her playgroup for parents of multiples across the bridge in Foster. Belle loved the women her brother and cousin had married, but really, she could do with a little less of the interference they liked to call girl time.

The poor man was new in town, and her sisters-in-law—her cousins were practically her brothers as they'd grown up in the same house—had already decided that he was perfect for her. She glanced at the bleachers where she had left the kids talking horse conformation. The judging team had wanted to meet despite the weather. "Jazz, what's the latest on the weather report?"

Phone in hand, Jazz frowned at her screen. "It doesn't look good. They've increased the chance of high winds and heavy rain." Her dark curls bounced when she twisted her head to survey the kids. "Possible hail. Should we call parents for an early pickup?"

Before Belle could respond, thunder rattled the walls of the arena. Then a bolt of lightning struck too close for comfort, blinding her.

The mare reared, forcing Belle to stay clear of the hooves. Her boot stuck in the deep sand and she stumbled.

Strong hands wrapped around her forearms, balancing her from behind.

Her lungs froze. Like the scared horse, she wanted to lash out, but the hands were gone just as quick.

"Are you okay?" A man's deep voice, low and calm, washed over her.

Belle kept her back to the stranger. She closed her eyes and took a steadying breath.

She was being ridiculous. It wasn't him, her ex, so she would move on as if nothing had happened. She focused on the young mare. The soft muzzle twitched with heavy pants. "Nothing's going to hurt you. It's okay, girl."

The mare's nostrils flared, and her ears flicked.

"Quinn!" Jazz's voice was a little on the overenthu-siastic side.

This must be the poor guy.

"Belle, this is Quinn Sinclair. He has twin daugh-ters who want to join the horse club. They're interested in the horse-judging team. Quinn, this is our fearless leader and my sister-in-law, Belle De La Rosa. Cassie and Lucy are her daughters."

The man stepped away from her and moved to the other side of the horse, looking at her over Little Lady's withers. "It's a pleasure to meet you. My daughters, Meg and Hannah, are in Cassie's Sunday school class." He ran a large hand over the mare's rump. "Need some help?"

They hadn't embellished his good looks. He was tall with classic features. His hair was dark blond with streaks of gold from being outside.

Good looks and an easy smile couldn't be trusted. That took the humor right out of her. Just like her ex-husband. All charm, but as nasty as a rattler when you got too close.

The grin on her sister-in-law's face was bright enough to put the lightning to shame. "I'm so happy you're here." Jazz turned that beaming face to Belle. "He can help with the horses, and I'll start calling parents to pick up early." She looked at Quinn. "Is that okay with you?"

"Sure." His answer was clear and confident.

No one bothered to ask her if she needed help. "I'm fine with the horses."

The rain pounded harder as strong winds pushed water under the edges of the large covered arena. Quinn moved closer to the nervous mare's head and brushed her muzzle. His hands were gentle as he calmed her.

"She's a beauty. At least we're not at the open arena. You have your hands full with this small herd."

She ignored his friendly chatter. They had probably told the poor man outrageous stuff about her to get him interested. Or made her sound like a charity case.

"Looks like parents have started to arrive," Quinn observed. "My girls were excited about the horse-judging team. They've never been in anything like that. Do they need experience? We don't own horses, much to their displeasure." He flashed her a smile, and her feminine side, dormant for years, woke up and paid attention.

Settle down, girl. What had he asked? Oh, yeah, horses. "Most of the kids don't. That's why I bring these guys. Some of the kids just want to be around a horse. I'll talk to your girls as soon as I get Lady in the trailer with Captain. He'll keep her calm. I don't want her panicking and hurting herself or any of the kids."

Jazz slipped her phone into her pocket and leaned close to Belle's ear. "Smile! Don't be so grumpy." Her voice was low, excited. "He's the one Selena wanted you to meet. He's cute, right?"

Belle rolled her eyes, then glanced at Quinn to make sure he hadn't overheard.

Of course, he had. He had his head down, but the quirk at the corner of his mouth was a giveaway.

Great. Were they trying to embarrass her? What had she done to deserve this torture? Just because they were happily married didn't mean she was missing out on anything.

She'd set them straight later. Of course, she'd done that before, and they'd ignored her.

Heading to the group of kids, Jazz waved at him. "Thanks for your help, Quinn."

He nodded, then smiled. Belle sighed. Of course he was better looking when he smiled. The long lines that cut into his cheeks were too perfect.

The horses needed her full attention. The poor mare's muscles were quivering under her beautiful roan coat.

"The girls have been excited since Cassie invited them to join the horse club at church a few weeks ago. Selena seemed thrilled. She said you're the best with kids and horses."

"Thanks." Of course Selena was thrilled. Belle sighed again. The last thing she needed was to encourage her sisters-in-law's matchmaking schemes or lead him on. "Sorry about Jazz and Selena. I find it best if I ignore them when they get…pushy."

"That's okay. Family, a blessing and a mess. They tend to think they know what's best. But it's all out of love. What can I do to help?"

That had to be a trick. She waited for Quinn to tell her what she needed to do or how she was doing it wrong. "I'm going to load Little Lady into the trailer, but I don't want to leave her alone. If you could follow with Cap, that would help. He's the big bay. With him by her side, she'll be settled." She headed off.

Without an argument, he did as she asked, leading the big guy to her with confidence that spoke of his familiarity with horses. He stopped at the trailer. "Are you ready for us?"

"Bring him in."

The trailer shifted as he loaded the gelding. Belle took the lead and secured him. "Thanks."

Quinn exited and waited for her at the gate. Once out, Belle slid the latch into place.

He nodded over his shoulder. "What about the other three horses?"

She had planned to use them for the demo tonight, but now it might be easier to load the trailer and be ready to leave. A couple of parents had already picked up their kids.

A gust of wind pushed up under the metal roof. "I should get them all in and settled."

"How far are you driving? This weather's getting ugly."

"I've handled worse. I've helped evacuate with a hurricane barreling down on us."

He raised his eyebrows. "That had to be terrifying. Which one do you want next? Do they have an order they travel in?"

"They do." And that he knew to ask shouldn't impress her. "Clyde's next."

They worked together to walk the rest of the horses into the trailer. She reached to shut the gate, but he was already swinging it closed.

She took a deep breath and reminded herself he was behaving like her brother or cousins would. It was not a personal insult to her abilities.

They joined Jazz with the kids.

There were a couple of children left. "Thank you for the help. We're good," she told him. "You should take your girls home."

He placed a black cowboy hat on his head and rested one boot on the bench next to the twin girls she had met earlier. Were they his? He leaned forward, arms crossed over his knee, and glanced at the trailer then her with a frown. "You're driving the five-horse trailer alone?"

"No, I have Cassie and Lucy." *Don't be insulted.*

The crease lines around his blue eyes deepened. "So, you're driving with two kids and five horses? How far? Someone should follow you at least."

A siren sounded from Main Street, heading toward the other side of town. She said a quick prayer, then looked at her wannabe hero.

The one she didn't need.

Why couldn't men see she was accomplished at handling whatever life threw at her? Either they had a hard time seeing her as competent enough to take care of herself and her girls, or they didn't see her at all. She wasn't sure which was worse.

She smiled; it was tight, but she didn't growl. Yay, her. "I'm more than capable of getting the horses and my girls home."

"I didn't mean to imply you couldn't—"

"Izabella!" Everyone turned at the booming voice.

She tilted her head and groaned. Xavier was stomping across the arena. Her cousin had been away for three years but still treated her like a little sister who needed protecting.

"What are you and Jazz still doing here? You should be at home and locked down. I'll follow you out to the ranch."

From the corner of her eye, she saw Quinn straighten and cross his arms. His lips twitched as if trying to suppress a grin. Complete failure on his part.

"We had to make sure all the kids were picked up and safe. I couldn't just take off. The horses are loaded, and as soon as the last kid is gone, I'm heading to the ranch."

Tanner Hernandez jumped up. "My dad's here. Bye, Ms. Belle."

Now they were down to her family and Quinn's.

The identical twins had to be his daughters. They had his sharp blue eyes, but the resemblance stopped there. Their thick dark lashes were so long they looked fake, and their perfectly straight, sleek black hair fell to the middle of their backs.

They were fine-boned and delicate. Their matching features created a picture of sweetness and innocence straight out of a fairy tale. Then they smiled. *Wow.*

She glanced at Quinn. They had to look like their mother. If that was the kind of woman he was attracted to, her sisters-in-law's matchmaking plot had never stood a chance.

She was about as opposite as a woman could get. Towering over the girls, she wiped her hands on her filled-out jeans before offering one to them. "Hi. Meg and Hannah, right?" She had met them briefly before the meeting started. "I'm so glad you could make it. Sorry about not getting to work with the horses tonight. Next time, okay?"

They nodded, their movements synchronized.

Jazz introduced Xavier to Quinn.

"Mom." Cassie took Belle's hand and smiled the smile that meant she wanted something. "Since we didn't get to go to the horse club, can they come home with us and spend the night?"

The twins' eyes filled with joy. They turned to their dad, hope in full force. "Could we?"

"Please?" all three girls said as one.

He started shaking his head no, and the girls' faces instantly fell.

It had to be hard to be the new girls in a small town, with all the friendships long ago established in preschool. Her heart went out to them. She knew too well the feeling of wanting to belong. "Hey, how about if they go with me? You could follow to make sure we all get there safe and sound. You can check out the house and come back in the morning. I make a pretty mean breakfast."

"That she does." Xavier rubbed the head of her youngest daughter, Lucy. "Her cinnamon rolls alone are worth the trip."

Belle hit him in the arm.

"What did I do?"

Ignoring him, she turned to Quinn. His girls hadn't said another word, but...*those eyes*. How did he ever tell them no?

Then again, she imagined he didn't hear no very often, either. Which reinforced the reason she needed to stay clear of him. Not the kind of man she wanted to be interested in. Not that she wanted to be interested in any man.

He hugged his daughters close and smiled at her again.

Quinn relaxed his gritted teeth. His first instinct was to tell them no. He never let them spend the night away. Then again, they were nine; the age other girls had sleepovers and made friends.

Plus, there was the matter of Belle De La Rosa. He knew there was matchmaking on the brains of some of the women in the playgroup. It happened every time he moved to a new town.

Married folks didn't like seeing single people run around unattached, even if said single people insisted that they were perfectly happy with the situation. He didn't want to get involved, to start over and drag his kids through the uncertainty of a new relationship.

Belle De La Rosa stood her ground with confidence and assurance. He'd never met a woman like her. She was almost as tall as him, her features strong, but in a stunning way he would never have expected he would be drawn to.

But it didn't matter. He was not on the market, and she'd made it clear she had no interest in him. Maybe it was her lack of interest that intrigued him.

Women weren't usually so fast at shooting him down. It was always the other way around.

He grinned and blamed his fascination on a wounded ego.

"Daddy." Meg's big eyes were pleading. She stepped away from him so that she could meet him eye to eye.

He sighed. "Okay. I'll—" They cheered before he could finish his sentence.

Xavier patted him on the shoulder. "Good. I'll make sure Jazz gets home safe, and I'll leave Belle to you." He grinned.

Belle slammed her fists on her hips. "Not you, too. This is ridiculous." She turned to Quinn. "I'm sorry about my family. Just ignore them. For the most part, they're harmless."

Her cousin didn't look harmless. He stood well over six feet, and his arms alone could do damage. It was clear that no one with a brain would mess with him or his loved ones. "Let me call my mother-in-law and tell her I'll be a little late."

He stepped away from the small group. The girls were chatting excitedly about sharing clothes. Oh, they'd need a change of clothes. The call went to voice mail.

He frowned and looked at the screen. She always answered. He tried again.

His heart raced. Gina was alone with Jonah. Thoughts swirled of all the possibilities. His son was only four; if something happened to his grandmother, he wouldn't know what to do.

Another call came in. It was a local area code. No one around here had a reason to call him this late.

Controlling his breath, he answered. "Quinn here."

"Oh, Quinn. I was having a hard time remembering your number." He relaxed a little at the sound of his mother-in-law's voice. "We're fine, but there's been a little accident."

The calm was short-lived. "Where's Jonah? What kind of accident? Why are you calling on someone else's phone?" A million worst-case scenarios ran through his brain. He knew how life could change in one blinding second.

The rain slammed against the roof as the wind picked up. He couldn't hear what she said. "Where are you?" His instinct to get in the Land Rover and go to them needed to be controlled. He needed facts. Then he would know what to do next.

"The sheriff has us in his car. He's very nice." Her accent started slipping through. She'd been eight when her grandparents had brought her to the States from Japan. Her accent surfaced only when she was tired or anxious.

He wanted to yell at her, but she was talking, so it couldn't be that bad. "What happened?"

"Well, I'm not sure. Lightning maybe? But there's a little fire at the back of the house. I dropped my phone when I grabbed Jonah. You aren't breathing, are you? Son, the important part is that we are okay. So, breathe."

No, he wasn't breathing. His son had been in danger, and he hadn't been there to keep him safe. For a moment, fear of what could have happened gripped him. He had promised his wife that he'd always protect their children. She had died holding their newborn son in her arms.

Now he had two jobs: take care of their family and grow the Yamazaki Marine Foundation, his wife's legacy. His mother-in-law trusted him with the foundation her husband had started, which had then been expanded under Quinn's wife's leadership.

"Quinn. We're safe and waiting for you here with the nice sheriff. Bye." She hung up.

He stared at his phone. Gina Yamazaki, his mother-in-law, was counting on him for so much, maybe more than he could accomplish. His wife and her father had been geniuses, way above anything he could do. But with them gone, it was up to him to continue the work they'd begun.

Protecting the oceans around the world hadn't just been a job for them; it had been their life's passion. His father-in-law had sold the family business and put all his wealth into the Foundation.

Quinn glanced at the woman who had stirred unexpected thoughts and gritted his teeth. He needed to stay focused on the job. Distractions were dangerous all the way around.

Chapter Two

A gentle touch brought Quinn back to the arena. Thunder rumbled, sounding farther away than earlier.

Concern had Belle's forehead creased. "Is everything okay?"

He lowered his voice so his girls wouldn't hear. "There's a fire at my house."

Belle's startled gasp caught everyone's attention. She waved off their questioning glances. "It's okay." Her grip on his arm tightened. She leaned closer. "Do you need to go?" she asked in a hushed voice. "Everyone's fine, right?"

He nodded. "My mother-in-law and son are with the sheriff. I don't know anything other than that. I need to make sure they're safe." He glanced at his girls.

"They can still go with me. I'll have Xavier follow us out, and I'll call you as soon as we get there." She held out her hand. "Give me your phone and I'll put my number in your contacts. I won't say anything to them. Is there anything else I can do?"

"Find me a place to live?" he half joked. His kids were homeless in the middle of a storm.

Sorry, Kari. His wife had been gone for almost five years now, but it seemed that every time he turned around, he was finding new ways to disappoint her. He jabbed his fists deep into his jacket pockets, fighting the need to rush out of here, but there was nothing he could do. He gritted his teeth. The girls needed to be in a safe place, too.

"That rental was hard enough to find." He watched her fingers type her number into his phone. They were strong hands, capable. But gentle when she was soothing a scared horse or a terrified man.

"I might be able to help you with that. We have a few bunkhouses and cabins on the ranch. We're on the Diamondback Ranch."

His breath seized somewhere between his lungs and his throat. She couldn't have said what he thought she said.

"We are a bit out of town, but as you've pointed out, there aren't many options in Port Del Mar."

Right. It would be ironic if he ended up living there. Should he tell her that was the reason he was in town? He hadn't gathered all the facts yet, but the Diamondback Ranch had one of the longest privately owned beaches on the Texas side of the Gulf Coast. And it wasn't developed yet. He was here to ensure it never would be.

Jazz joined them, cutting off anything he might say. "What's going on?"

"There's been an emergency at Quinn's house. I'm taking the girls to the ranch." Her gaze sought his. "Right?"

He nodded.

"What kind of emergency?" Jazz asked. "Is it medical? Should you go with him?"

He broke eye contact with Belle and looked at Jazz in confusion.

The petite woman pointed to Belle. "She's one of our county's backup EMTs and an official Red Cross volunteer. She's not on call tonight, but she's the perfect person to have on-site. Xavier and I can drive the girls and horses to the ranch."

Belle's hand tightened on his bicep again. The contact shouldn't have comforted him. "Will that work? I can go with you."

"Yeah. I need to be there. She says they're fine, but—"

"I get it."

Quinn pulled out his keys to unlock his Land Rover and was surprised to see his hands shaking. He had lost the stupid key fob a few months ago. He should have taken the time to replace it.

Belle had gone to get something out of her truck and was now talking to her girls. Raising her head, she made eye contact with him. The keys fell out of his grip. Picking them up, he tried unlocking his door again.

She hugged her daughters, then joined him. Her steady hand gently covered his trembling one. "I'll drive. It'll be safer." Then she opened the driver's door and climbed in behind the wheel.

"I can—"

"I know you can. But your focus is on your family right now. Mine would be, too. Let me focus on the road and get us there safely."

He gave her his address, then rushed to the passenger side. As soon as he was in, she was moving. "EMT.

Red Cross. Animal rescue. When you said you could take care of yourself, you were being modest. It seems you can take care of everyone."

With a shrug, she kept her eyes on the wet roads. "Running a ranch and raising two girls alone in a small rural community kind of forces one to be self-sufficient. There's always someone who needs help. It feels good to provide it."

The wipers cut back and forth, but the rain was coming down so hard they couldn't keep up. He wanted to ask her about the beach that ran along her ranch, but he wasn't ready to explain why he was in town. Locals had been known to react badly when they found out he was trying to stop development. But he also didn't want to get information without her knowing who he was. That wouldn't be fair.

She cared so much for her community. Maybe she cared about the land, too.

He didn't want this to turn into a small-town conflict.

"Maybe it's not that bad, and you can stay in the house," she said.

One could hope. "She said it was only in the back."

Turning the steering wheel hand over hand, she drove down his street. Flashing lights from first-response vehicles lit the night. Smoke billowed over the neighborhood. The bright colors of the three-story coastal homes were muted in the stormy night.

She moved in behind a fire truck, but before she came to a complete stop, he was out of the SUV.

Everything inside him went still. As usual, his mother-in-law was the queen of understatement. It was not a small fire. Half of the house was gone. Nothing but a blackened shell stood where the girls' rooms had been.

The front of the house looked untouched. But even he could see it was a total loss. The support beams had to be compromised.

Gina and Jonah had been in there when the fire started. His muscles locked.

Firefighters and police were everywhere. He scanned the area for his mother-in-law. She had Jonah. He needed to see them. Hold them.

"Mr. Sinclair?" A tall officer in a tan cowboy hat approached. "I'm Sheriff Cantu. Your son and mother are over here."

He didn't bother to correct the man. Gina often introduced herself as his mother. They were in the sheriff's SUV. Jonah was cocooned in a blanket, his cheek resting against his grandmother's chest. Tears streaked his face.

Opening the door, he wrapped his son in his arms and pressed him close. Their hearts matched up. "Shhh. It's okay. I've got you, little man."

"Daddy, a big bang hit our house and woke me up. It's on fire. Buck is inside."

He laid his lips against the top of his son's silky black hair. The faint smell of smoke replaced the usual clean scent of his apple shampoo. "We'll get you a new Buck." The floppy toy pony had been with Jonah since his birth.

Kari had bought it for him. Quinn closed his eyes tight against the grief. "You and Baba are safe. That's all that matters." The stoic expression was barely covering the distress in his mother-in-law's face. "How are you, Baba?" He had fallen into the habit of calling her by the grandmother title.

The rain stopped hitting him. Glancing up, he saw a

huge rainbow umbrella. Behind it was Belle. The blue and red lights flashed across her face.

The sheriff moved closer to her. "Hey, Belle. I thought Miguel was on Red Cross duty tonight."

"He is. But the father and his two girls were with me at the arena. Please, let Miguel know I've got them covered. They'll be at the ranch if anyone needs to talk to them."

"Sure thing. We almost lost the whole street, but the rain helped control the fire." He nodded to Quinn. "Sorry about your loss." Then he moved toward the fire truck.

Belle leaned into the SUV and held her free hand out to Gina. "Hello, I'm Izabella De La Rosa. I'm with the Red Cross, and I have a warm, dry place for y'all to stay tonight."

Gina took the offered hand. "Thank you. I'm Gina Yamazaki." She looked at Quinn. "The girls?"

"They're with Belle's daughters. We'll be following them," he reassured her.

"We should go now. They won't let you close to the house tonight. My kids are about the same size as yours, so we'll have everything you need. My brother and cousins keep a change of clothes at the ranch." Carefully holding the huge umbrella over them, she guided them to his Land Rover. The rain soaked her clothing. He wanted to hand Jonah to Gina and make sure Belle was under cover, too, but he doubted she would appreciate his offer.

As they made their way back to his car, he kept his gaze away from the house they had moved into less than a month ago. His goal was to get to know the people of the community and the land. Right now, he wanted his family in one safe place where he could see them and hold them.

With everyone secured, they drove out of town.

"I smell like smoke," Gina said from the back, next to a now sleeping Jonah. Turning in his seat, Quinn reached over and placed a hand on her knee. Order and control were her happy places. She twisted her wedding ring as she stared out the window.

Belle made brief eye contact. "It's been a trying night. Once you get settled in the cabin, you can take a nice, warm shower. Jazz is more your size, Gina. She has some extra clothes at the ranch that will fit you. The cabins are one room with a loft. There's a double in the room with two bunk beds upstairs, and the sofa folds out into a bed. There's only one bathroom, but it's big. We'll get the kitchen stocked for you. You'll be able to stay as long as you need."

"How much longer until we're there?"

"We're about twenty minutes out of town. Another fifteen, and we'll be there. It's the Diamondback Ranch."

Her eyes went big. "Diamondback? Is that the—"

"It's your family's ranch?" He didn't want Gina to say too much yet. Not until he could figure out what direction they were going to go. There was a lot of shoreline to explore, and her ranch was a part of it. How much of a part?

She took some time answering. He wasn't sure if it was the weather she was driving through or the question.

"Yes. Frank De La Rosa ran it for the last twenty-five years, but he passed away recently. It's complicated. He was my uncle—my mother's brother—but raised

my brother and me along with his kids. If you had any
dealings with him, I'll apologize so we can move on."

Quinn studied the woman driving. This was not
going to go well. "We did know of Frank. I had spoken
with him on the phone several times." He had not been
a pleasant man and had been putting roadblocks up.

Belle kept her focus on the road. The rain and winds
had settled a bit, but it was still rough going. Why would
he have had business with her uncle? Did they owe him
money, and he was here to collect? Or was it worse?
With her uncle, there was no telling.

Her stomach roiled. Everything was still unsettled
with the ranch. They were at risk of losing it.

With her uncle's death and her mother and cousin
missing, the estate was a mess. Her mother owned part
of it, but they hadn't been able to find her. It had been
over twenty years since she'd abandoned Belle and Elijah, and there'd been little contact since. For all they
knew, the woman was dead.

Don't borrow trouble where there is none. She took
a deep breath to settle the nausea before it got out of
control.

"Jazz said you'd been in town for almost a month.
What brings you to Port Del Mar?" What she really
wanted to know was the reason he had spoken with
Frank.

"Business. I work in Houston with agencies that deal
with marine conservation. Port Del Mar is small, but it's
a rich environment for many of our endangered species
and fragile communities."

Okay, that didn't sound like it had anything bad to
do with her uncle.

"So how long will you be staying?" She glanced at his son. "Cassie and Lucy didn't say anything about seeing your kids in school. It's a very small school, but we're able to attract top-notch educators due to our lifestyle. People love the opportunity to live on the coast."

"Each assignment is different. This one looks to be six months or so. Due to my work, it's easier to homeschool."

"Oh. There's also a very active homeschool group. You probably already know that."

"Yeah. They've been very welcoming." He turned and checked on his son and mother-in-law again. He reached out and touched the older woman's hand. She gripped it, but neither said a word.

The fact that he was so close to his mother-in-law said a lot about the man. It had to be death and not divorce that had separated him from his wife.

Thunder rattled the night, and Belle fixed her gaze on the road ahead. At least he wasn't here because of some dark deal with her uncle. The last thing she needed right now was more complications with the ranch. She was barely hanging on as it was.

Quickly lifting a prayer of thanksgiving, she stopped the negative thoughts before they became a spiral of doom. There was so much to be grateful for. Her girls were healthy and happy. Their father wouldn't be a threat any longer. He had built a life in another state.

More important, Xavier was home and Elijah was sober and reunited with his wife and daughter. The people she loved were safe and close in her orbit.

"You'll be able to stay in the cabin as long as you need. It's not as big as the house you rented, but long-term rentals are impossible to find. If it won't work for you, there are more options across the bridge. It's not that far of a drive."

"I like to stay in the community where I'm doing the work. Plus, we're water people. The closer to the water we are, the happier we are. Most of my childhood summers were spent in South Padre. Plus, my kids are used to being close to the ocean."

Gina leaned forward. "My husband started the Yamazaki Marine Foundation in Houston. Then my daughter took over when we lost him. Now Quinn runs it. The ocean has always been a family mission."

Lightning danced across the sky, but it was in the distance now. The rumbling of the thunder subdued as she turned into the ranch. A trumpet blared into the car, and Quinn pulled his phone out of his pocket.

"That'll get your attention," she laughed, after her racing heart settled.

"It's the girls." He lifted the phone to his ear. "Everything okay?"

He waited a bit. "Yes, we're staying on the ranch. Baba and Jonah are fine, but there was a fire at the house. It's going to be okay. We're at the ranch entryway. I'll explain everything when we get there. It should be soon."

"Less than five minutes," Belle told him.

He smiled and nodded at her. "Okay. Yes. Baba and Jonah are fine. I'll let her know. I love you more. See you in a minute." With a heavy sigh, he lowered the phone. "Mr. De La Rosa said to meet him at Cabin Two."

She frowned. "Mr. De La Rosa?" He knew her uncle was dead. "Oh, Xavier?" She laughed. "I've never heard him referred to as 'Mr.'"

"He owns the ranch now, right?"

"His father was Frank, so he and Damian have more rights to the ranch than I do. My grandfather gave seventy-five percent to his son and twenty-five percent to his daughter, my mother." She tightened her lips. Why was she offering him information?

"But you run it?"

From the corner of her eye, she saw the intensity of his eyes as he studied her. "I manage the ranch. The daily running. We're trying to locate my mother so that we can…" She wanted to slam her head against the steering wheel. She didn't talk family business with anyone. If she did, she'd have to explain why they were trying to get their mother taken off all family holdings. She didn't want to say that she couldn't trust the woman who gave birth to her. It was humiliating. "And Gabby. She's Frank's youngest. She was sent to live with a great-aunt after her mother, Frank's wife, died. We've lost touch with her."

He didn't need to know that her brothers had sent her away at the age of nine to protect her from her own father.

She had worked hard to change the reputation of the De La Rosa family. Her daughters, niece and nephews were not going to grow up as laughingstock of the county like her and the boys.

She was proud of all her brother and cousins had overcome, and she was going to make sure the ranch stayed in the family and flourished.

That was a full-time job. The last time she'd allowed good looks and a charming smile to distract her with dreams of another life, it hadn't ended well. Her hand lightly touched the mark along the side of her temple.

Unfortunately, she had the scars to prove it.

Just because he was nice to his mother-in-law and obviously loved his kids didn't change the fact that she wasn't interested. She wasn't.

Chapter Three

As the sun touched the land the next morning, Belle turned the horses out. She stood at the fence and watched them run. The air was fresh with wet earth, and the sky was clear. No sign of the storm.

She hadn't ridden the southwest pastures in a while.

Fence day was on her schedule this morning. Starting her daily ritual, she patted the post next to her as she spoke to it. "Oh, Guardians of the Pastures, it's time to visit your brothers-in-arms in a faraway land."

She rolled her eyes at herself. *Really, Izabella, you need more time with adults.* This was what happened to someone who didn't have time for people.

Selena might be right to worry about her holding conversations with objects. At least they weren't answering back yet.

"Mom!" Cassie came running around the barn with her five-year-old sister and Frog, their Australian shepherd, close on her heels. That dog rarely left their sides. "We did our morning inside chores. Can we go to Cabin Two? We want to show Meg and Hannah the baby goats."

Lucy nodded, her dark curls flying around her face. "And the chickens."

Belle waved Lucy over to her and slipped the rubber band off her wrist and onto her daughter's unruly hair. "It's early and Meg and Hannah had a long night. Feed the chickens and gather the eggs. I'll cook some breakfast and, before we feed the goats, I'll call and see if they want to come over. They have a lot to deal with, so I'm not sure what their dad wants to do."

Lucy pouted. Cassie's shoulders slumped. "But they wanted to feed the baby goats and I told them they could help. They were super excited."

Before she could say anything, her phone vibrated in her pocket. "Girls, I'm not arguing about this. The chickens are waiting for you."

Heads down, they moved to the henhouse as if they'd lost their puppies. She shook her head. So dramatic.

Her phone vibrated again. It was Quinn. "Hi, Quinn. Sorry, I was distracted."

"No problem. I assumed that running a ranch you'd be up already. The girls are driving me crazy saying that they're supposed to help bottle-feed baby goats this morning. Do you know anything about this?"

She laughed. "We're going to have to watch our girls very carefully. They're plotters. Poor Jonah doesn't have a chance. Cassie told me they'd asked to help feed the goats."

He groaned. "I'm sorry. I'll talk to them about inviting themselves."

"I'm pretty sure Cassie organized all of this. She has a knack. I know you have a lot to deal with today. Why don't you bring them over to the house? In another hour I'll have breakfast ready. You and Gina can join us. The kids can hang out with me today while you take care of the house."

"Three extra kids? That's a lot."

"Nah. Around here, that's the norm. Yours are all potty trained and can feed themselves. That's a bonus. You remember Xavier? He has triplets. Two-year-old triplets. And my brother's little girl is here all the time, too. She's six. Yours will fit in fine, and if they don't, I promise to call."

"So, it's okay if we come over?"

"Sure. In fact, I'll be driving past your place, so I can pick you up—I have to drop some mail off to Damian."

"Damian?"

"Yes. Another De La Rosa. We're everywhere. Xavier's younger brother. He lives in the farthest cabin."

"Okay."

With a slight shift in plans, Belle loaded the girls into the old Suburban, gathered the Sinclair clan and went by Damian's. As usual, her cousin was sitting on the porch, looking as though he were on guard. His two Belgian Malinois sat on either side of him. She hadn't even heard of the dog breed until he'd come back from the army with one. Now he had two. They were as silent and stoic as their master.

"Stay here. I'm going to give Damian his mail. He doesn't like strangers."

As she climbed out, she heard Lucy say, "He likes horses and dogs. He doesn't like people at all."

She shook her head. Were they making it worse, letting Damian hide from the world? Everyone was afraid to force the issue. He was safe out here. But was it enough? Would he ever be happy?

A few words, very few, and they were on their way

to the barns. Once inside, she loved the sound of all the childish giggles as they took turns bottle-feeding the four goats. A local rancher had given them to her to hand-raise after their mother had abandoned them.

The morning flew by. Before she knew it, all the chores were done, and breakfast was eaten. As she made her way to the stables, Elijah joined her to help check the fences.

Jazz and her daughter, Rosie, were hanging out until after lunch. Then Jazz would be heading to town for a meeting.

The best part was that Gina had volunteered to watch the kids for the rest of the day. Her girls didn't have grandparents of their own, so they were eating up the attention and already calling her Baba. She would be added to the list of adopted grandparents her girls were collecting. They craved family connections, and Belle was grateful that Xavier's and Elijah's in-laws accepted her daughters, too.

Out in the pastures with Elijah, she discovered that the storm had caused more damage than she'd predicted, and they didn't get home until the sun was close to the western horizon. Horses put away, Elijah headed for his truck, and she went to the back porch. Gina was in a rocker, reading.

"Sorry. We're later than I thought we'd be. Have you heard from Quinn?"

Looking over her glasses, she nodded. "My car is totaled, but the insurance company is being difficult. Everything in the kids' rooms is a total loss." She shook her head. "Every time I start thinking of all the little things we lost, I get overwhelmed, so I'm reading.

We're all safe and have a place to stay. Thank you for your help."

"*De nada.* Reading's a good strategy. It's one of my favorites. Where are the kids? Are they inside?"

"They watched a movie, then asked to go out to the garden." She pointed to the large area surrounded by the tall fence.

As Belle headed toward the garden, she planned out the next week in her head. She reflected that ranch work was hard, but it recharged her heart, mind and body. She reached the garden gate. "Cassie?"

No answer. "Lucy?"

She stood in the center of the garden and listened. Five kids should make some noise. "Cassie. Lucy. I'm tired and not in the mood for hide-and-seek." They loved hiding in the garden. The walls of green bean runners and bamboo teepees were not yet covered with cucumber vines, but it still made for cozy hiding places. It was early in the season, and plants weren't as solid as they'd be in another month.

They weren't there. Had they gone inside without Gina seeing them?

She walked through the garden again. It was a quarter of an acre, so there was some space to cover.

She called their names. The back gate was open. Her heart fluttered. Her girls knew better than to take off away from the house without adult permission.

But they had new friends to impress. Standing outside the garden, she called all their names. There was a path that went to the barns. Maybe they had gone to play with the goats.

Her dog was missing, too. That made her feel a little better. That dog would be barking like crazy if anything was wrong. Jogging to the goat barn, she rushed through the doors, calling their names. Nothing.

Don't panic. They're here somewhere. The chickens. Kids found chicks irresistible. Deep breaths and long strides got her to the large chicken coop. No kids.

It was time to call for help. Elijah wouldn't be too far out, and she needed to call Quinn. Maybe the kids had gone to the cabin.

On the way back to the house, she called her brother. He immediately turned around. Then she called Quinn. She'd promised him his kids would be safe with her. She wanted to throw up.

Gina was still in the rocker. Her chin was down as if she was sleeping.

"Gina." Belle shook her gently on the shoulder.

Sitting straight up, the older woman blinked to clear her eyes. "Everything all right?"

"The kids left the garden. I went to the barns, but they weren't there. They might have gone to the cabin. Elijah's on his way, and I left a message for Quinn. I'm going to walk to your cabin on the back path. My girls would have known about the path connecting the house to the cabins. You stay here and keep an eye out. Tell Elijah and Quinn where I am. One of them should drive to the cabin. The other can follow me on the path. Okay?"

Oh, no. Tears were forming in Gina's eyes. "I thought they'd be okay in the garden." She stood. "Let me help find them."

"I need you to stay here. Elijah and Quinn are coming here, and I might miss the kids if they come back to the house. So, stay here."

Gina walked to the railing and scanned the area. "Okay."

Jumping off the porch, Belle dashed to the back of the garden and slowly started tracking the path they'd have taken if they'd gone to the cabin.

Cassie was old enough to understand the dangers. What had led them to leave the garden? Something moved behind her. Heart pounding, she turned. Someone was walking through the thicket. Someone larger than a child.

Belle crouched, putting herself in a better position to run or charge depending on what was needed. She had her knife on her belt, but no gun.

The thicket was pushed back, and she saw a black cowboy hat. Clear blue eyes met hers. Quinn.

She stood and sighed. "I'm so happy to see you. You got here really fast."

His mouth was tight. "I was pulling up to the house when you left the message. My phone is off while I'm driving. Gina sent me this way. Have you seen the kids? How long have they been missing?"

Returning to the trail, she glanced over her shoulder at him. "Less than forty-five minutes, longer than thirty." Her phone vibrated. "Elijah sent a message. He's driving straight to the cabin. If they're not there, he'll get Damian and Xavier on horseback, and they'll cover more ground. But I think we'll find them between here and the cabin." She pointed to some of the shrubs. "The branches are broken, and grass is trampled here."

She stopped. The thicket was pushed back. "It looks like someone went off-trail." Crouching, she pushed her way through the smaller area. She was too big for this.

"Did you find something?" He was right behind her.

"Cassie," she called. Her heart raced.

"Mama. Shhh. You'll scare them." Cassie's voice came from deep in the underbrush, somewhere to the left of her. Belle's faithful dog, Frog, was flat on her belly, pressed against Cassie. Her brown and blue eyes shifted, then looked away, guilty.

"Cassandra De La Rosa Perez!" She wanted to cry in relief and yell in anger all at the same time.

One of the twins came out of the thicket, her dark blue eyes shining with excitement. "We've been tracking kittens. They're lost and hungry. But every time we get close, they run again." She put her fingers to her lips. "They're getting tired. One keeps falling. We want to help them, but they're scared of us."

"Sweetheart, you know to leave animals alone. Their mother is probably looking for them. We were scared because you said you'd stay in the garden, but you didn't. Baba is scared and worried. I was worried. We have Cassie and Lucy's uncles looking for you."

The other twin came out holding her brother's hand. "Daddy, when you see them, you'll understand. They don't have a mother. They're super skinny, and they look sick and beat-up. They need help and we were the only ones around."

He groaned and tilted his head. "Even more of a reason not to follow them. You should have told Baba and waited for us." He went around Belle and knelt in front of his children. "You are in major trouble, and we will figure out a consequence. First, apologize to Ms. De La Rosa."

All three turned to her and said they were sorry for scaring her and leaving the garden.

"Where are these orphaned kittens?" she asked.

They turned and crouched to get through the thick undergrowth. Belle crawled through the little tunnel they had made to follow the kittens. Cassie was sitting with her knees pulled to her chest. Lucy was flat on her stomach. Her arms stretched out in front of her, reaching farther into an area Belle couldn't see due to the branches and plants.

"Lucy! What are you doing? There could be snakes or all sorts of things that could hurt y'all."

Cassie looked up at her. Big tears hovered in her gray-green De La Rosa eyes. "Mama. They're hurt and sick. Lucy's letting them get used to her so she can get close enough to grab them. Please, Mama. I know we should have told you, but they were running away, and if we didn't follow, we'd lose them." The tears fell. Her baby had the biggest heart.

Crawling her way to them, Belle grimaced, sure she was tearing and staining her clothes past repair as she made her way through the thick bush. "Where are they?"

Cassie pointed, and Belle looked through the branches of the shrubs. In a bed of dried leaves, two spotted kittens were curled around each other. The girls were right. They didn't look like they'd make it much longer.

Quinn was at her shoulder. A strange noise escaped his throat. "Oh, sweetheart. Those aren't domestic kittens. It looks like you found a pair of ocelots."

Turning, eyes wide, Belle looked at him. "Here? But they're endangered."

He leaned closer. "Yeah, just a handful left in the wild, and they like to hide. The girls are right. These guys have been orphaned."

Lucy wiggled closer. "I touched one," she whispered.

"Easy, baby." Belle put her hand on her youngest daughter's shoulder. "These are wild animals."

"But I can reach it now." Her voice hushed as she focused on the small cats.

After taking off his long-sleeved button-up, Quinn stretched out beside her. That was a major accomplishment. The space was small, and he wasn't. The undergrowth was cutting at his now bare arms. His cotton T-shirt didn't provide much protection.

"Can you slowly pull the cub closer to me?"

Lucy nodded, and with her tongue out in concentration, she gently brought the furball closer to them. Everyone held their breaths.

The furball hissed as he wrapped it in his shirt. "Okay. Good job. Can you get the other one?"

She nodded and moved deeper into the thicket. After a little wiggling and slow-motion movement, she handed the second one to him.

"They're both females," he said, carefully studying them. "They look dehydrated and malnourished, but they're definitely ocelots." His eyes shimmered with excitement. "De La Rosas, you have ocelots living on your ranch. It's amazing."

The kids crowded around him. "Can we keep them?"

"No. We can nurture them back to health, but they're wild animals and need to live in their natural habitat."

Jonah reached for one of the cats.

"Careful, son. You can look at them, but we don't want to handle them too much."

"We found them, and they don't have parents. We should keep them. We feed the baby goats and raise baby chickens." Cassie's eyes were gathering tears.

Belle took her daughter's hand. "Sweetheart, we have no clue what wildcats need."

"I'll call the local game warden and report the ocelots. They'll need to be released into the wild when they're old enough. But we might be able to nurse them until then."

"Daddy can do it. He's a doctor," one of Quinn's girls said.

Belle's head went from the tiny cats to his face. That was a surprise she didn't see coming.

"Hannah." His voice held a hint of warning. Then he glanced at Belle. "I'm not a medical doctor. I have a PhD in marine biology with a focus on coastal habitats. We can get these guys independent and back on their feet, then release them here on the ranch." When they made eye contact this time, he held it. Like he had something to say but didn't know how. "Belle, I'm not sure you understand the ramifications. This is a huge discovery."

He had a PhD and she'd gotten a GED. She had a hard time looking away from him. Could he see her lack of education? Did he just accuse her of being slow?

In the distance, she heard the rumbling of a truck. "Oh." Pulling her phone out, she dialed Elijah. "We need to call and let everyone know the kids are safe." With a hard glare at Cassie, she listened to the rings. "Young lady, we will be talking about y'all leaving without a word. There were better ways to handle this."

"Yes, ma'am."

Once she'd told Elijah the story, he said he'd contact everyone else.

"What's the best way to tell Gina?" she asked. "She lost her phone. Will she answer the ranch line?"

"I just gave her a new phone." He read out the number.

Belle could hear the tears in the poor woman's voice as she explained the situation. Hanging up, she shook her head. Quinn had moved the kids to the path and was slowly heading to the house.

Putting an arm around her daughter, who was too stubborn for her own good, Belle lowered her voice. "Cassie, do you understand how scared she was? How horrible it was when we couldn't find you? The first thing you will do is apologize to their grandmother."

Quinn glanced at her, his lips in a tight line. "Hannah. Meg. After last night, this was the last thing Baba needed."

So much for trying to keep it private. Cassie was clearly upset. "What about Lucy and Jonah? They left, too."

"They're little," both parents said at the same time.

Belle looked at her youngest. "But, Lucy, you know better, too. You don't leave the house area without an adult."

"Yes, ma'am."

One of the ocelots yawned and pushed a paw out of the shirt to touch Quinn's face. He gently rubbed the kitten's chin and said words so soft and low she couldn't hear.

Her heart melted. *No, Belle, it doesn't matter if he is the male equivalent of Snow White. You are not interested in him.*

The rest of the walk to the house was silent. Once there, Belle helped Quinn find a cozy box for the babies and helped him gather supplies to feed them.

Quinn firmly set limits on how close the kids could be to the sleeping ocelots. Now all five kids were flat on their stomachs in the living room, their chins resting on crossed arms as they watched the kittens as if they were the most interesting movie they'd ever seen.

"The kittens have to stay with us, because our daddy is the doctor." One of the twins was already building her case for custody.

"But it's our ranch and we've raised all sorts of animals." Cassie looked over her shoulder. "Right, Mama?"

"I saw them first, so they're ours," Lucy argued. She wiggled closer and Jonah mirrored her action.

"Thanks." Quinn put his phone in his pocket. The kids continued to debate shared custody, and Gina fussed over everyone, insisting she would feed them all.

"Belle." He reached for her hand to pull her away from the kids and cats.

She studied his hand interlocked with hers. His was so large it made her look feminine. That didn't happen often. They fit together well.

Normally she didn't like to be touched and withdrew, but he was different. Why?

She jerked her hand back.

"Are you all right?" It was either pity or curiosity in his gaze. She couldn't tell which.

Relaxing her shoulders and letting her arms drop, she smiled. "I don't like being touched. I was just caught by surprise."

"Sorry." He nodded his head at the kids. "I wanted to get out of earshot."

"Oh." Heat climbed her neck up to her cheeks. She could feel it but couldn't stop it. "What's up?"

"I spoke to the game warden. With my certification, I can keep the kittens until they're ready for release. Then I'll work with a local game preserve to make sure they're safe to return to the wild. You get to tell your girls." He went to the archway and looked into the living room, where the kids were lined up on the floor. "They won't be happy."

"No. But we really don't need another project, anyway. They'll be fine, and it will give them an excuse to visit your kids."

"I'd like to find a time to talk. How about dinner tomorrow night?"

"No. I don't do dinner."

He raised an eyebrow and looked at her as if she'd said something ridiculous.

"What? No one ever tells you no?"

Surprise etched his brow, but then he laughed. "I haven't asked anyone to dinner in a very long time. I was confused when you said you don't do dinner. As in, you have something against eating in the evening."

"Oh." Her cheeks burned again. "I eat dinner, just not with people. I mean, with men." She groaned. "I don't date. I want to be clear on the subject. I never go on dates."

With a nod, Quinn went in to gather his family.

She needed to stay as far away as possible. One finger caressed the ruined skin that ran along her temple. If she had any unruly thoughts about this man, she needed to remember that there was no Prince Charming in the real world. This Cinderella had to save herself.

Chapter Four

Baba's soothing voice drifted from the loft. She was reading to the kids in her native language. She'd also taught them Spanish, and last month she'd introduced them to German. She'd thought it best if the children weren't exposed to his Texas accent while they were in the developing stages. He grinned. For years she had politely tried to hide her shudder when he attempted to speak anything other than English.

His wife would be pleased. Kari had mastered seven languages and dabbled in several others.

She'd laughed at his attempts to speak Japanese, but it had been important to both of them that their children speak it.

He leaned his head back and closed his eyes, ignoring the book in his lap. As the familiar sounds washed over him, he searched for Kari's voice in his memories.

It was coming up on five years since he'd heard her laugh. That laugh had been the first thing that had drawn his attention to her. Like a fresh spring rain after a harsh drought, the sound had rolled across the campus library. He'd lost all concentration, and, in less than ten minutes, he'd found an excuse to join her table.

That moment had changed the direction of his life. In a very good way. He had been lost after the sudden death of his parents.

Quinn focused on his breathing. In less than a week, Jonah would turn five. The day would mark the date he'd held his son for the first time. And held his wife for the last.

His eyes burned as he worked to anchor her voice to the front of his brain.

That was where he wanted it, but it was slipping farther away, becoming less tangible each year. Forgetting her would be a travesty. She deserved better from him.

Everything good in his life was due to her. He'd still be an aimless surfer with too much useless education and no purpose if it hadn't been for her.

If only he'd been stronger and insisted she stay in the States…or he could have canceled his trip and stayed home. Someone else could have gone.

There had been options that wouldn't have led to her death on the side of a washed-out road in the jungles of a developing country. Because of him, she had died with only him next to her as she gave birth to their son.

All she had asked of him was to love their children enough for both of them. He had been useless, promising he'd love her forever, but she had still slipped from him.

He flexed his fingers and studied his hands. Useless.

They'd been single-minded in their goals and thought themselves invincible.

As passionate as she was about their mission, it hadn't been worth her life.

Abandoning the novel, he picked up the Bible on the side table. *God, hold me.* He flipped to Kari's favorite verse, John 14:27. *Peace I leave with you, my peace I give unto you: not as the world giveth, give I unto you. Let not your heart be troubled, neither let it be afraid.*

But he was afraid. He was afraid of Kari fading from his mind. His gut turned as another woman crossed his thoughts. A woman who was going to hate him when she learned why he was in town.

Slouching farther into the chair, he sighed. Tonight, prayer didn't help. An ugly rage at God hissed and clawed at him as he pushed it down. The anger only exposed his guilt. He should have been the one to die. Sitting up, he rubbed his temples. This train of thought was not good for anyone, especially his children. He had promised to put them first, always.

Soft rustling told him that Gina was descending the small spiral stairs. He helped her alight and tried to lead her to the room where she slept.

With a shake of her head, she quietly but stubbornly went to the kitchen to make tea. Biting back a groan, he sat in his chair. He wasn't in the mood to talk. If he were smart, he would pull out the sofa bed before she finished and pretend to be asleep, but it had become a habit for them to talk about the day before they called it a night.

"Quinn, son." Her voice was gentle, but there was no denying the hard edge. She wanted to talk, and they would not be going to sleep until he heard what was on her mind.

With a sigh, he lifted his head and smiled at her. So polite but headstrong, just like her daughter.

"Jonah's birthday will be here soon. Have you made

any plans? He's no longer a baby and will remember these days. Your actions or lack of them will be his childhood memories."

How did she do it? It was also the anniversary of her only child's death. A death that was his fault. Kari had been the better parent, partner, scientist. The better Christian. At times he wondered if God cared what happened down here at all. He tilted his head until the raw beams of the ceiling filled his view and cleared his thoughts.

They would only upset this dear woman. He didn't warrant her loyalty or love.

Shifting to be closer to her, he smiled. "Where did the time go? I can't believe it's been five years."

For a moment, there was a shine in her dark eyes.

Great. He was going to make her cry. She never cried.

The kettle whistled. Gina moved around the little kitchen and lined up her supplies. "Would you like some tea?"

"Yes, thank you." He'd already upset her enough tonight. "Gina, I'm sorry—"

"We can't be sad." Her back to him, she stood on tiptoe to pull two chunky mugs from the open cabinet.

He made a mental note to replace the delicate teacups she had lost to the fire. It wasn't much, but he could at least do that for her. She went through the process of making tea, each movement full of intent and purpose.

Handing a cup to him, she sat. "Ask Belle. She knows the area and has connections with many of the children. Maybe she can help set it up. We need to do something special for him." She leaned forward. "I know it's a difficult day, but it wasn't his fault."

"I know that." No, Kari's death was squarely on his shoulders alone. The man who had promised to love, honor and protect her. "I'll talk to Belle. I'm not sure she'll be able to help on such short notice or want to help us once I tell her we are here to stop any development along the beach."

He needed to talk to her about several things. The welcome they'd been enjoying on the ranch might be withdrawn.

Silence lingered as they each became lost in their own thoughts. After an hour, his mother-in-law gathered the cups and washed them. With a soft "Good night," she went to the bedroom.

He was so tired he thought about sleeping in the recliner. Checking his watch, he noted it was time to feed the baby ocelots. Then he'd check on his own babies.

The hungry ocelots quickly fell back to sleep after getting their milk.

In the loft, he found all three in one of the lower bunk beds. At least it was a double. He eyed the empty twin. Maybe he'd sleep up here with them. Hannah opened her sleepy eyes. "Jonah didn't want to sleep alone. He misses Buck. He couldn't decide who he wanted to sleep with. Did the babies eat?"

She was so much like her mother, always worried about everyone else. He leaned over and kissed her on the forehead, brushing her silky black hair. "Yes. They're all tucked in."

He slipped off his boots and lay down on the quilt that covered the empty bed. He watched as Hannah snuggled closer to Jonah. The boy was tucked in tightly between his sisters.

Quinn set his alarm but had a feeling the girls

wouldn't need him to wake them in time to feed the baby goats.

He'd thought marine biologists woke up early, but ranchers' morning hours were ridiculously inhuman. His eyes gave in, and sleep claimed him. He dreamed of a rancher who walked with a fierceness that dared the world to mess with her or the ones she loved. Dark wild curls fanned out around her as she swung onto a horse and took off.

In some ways she was the opposite of his wife; in other ways they were too much alike.

The bumps on the dirt road went right along with his foul mood. As the goat barn came into view, the happy chatter of his children contrasted starkly with the heavy cloud in his brain.

This time of year, as spring brought new life to the world around him, he struggled with dark emotions. He tried praying, but his thoughts bounced. He didn't want to admit it out loud, but he'd rather not talk to God.

Which only made matters worse. He needed to pull himself out of this funk before it bled over to his kids.

His hands gripped the steering wheel much tighter than necessary. How could his brain allow another woman to slip into his dreams? It was the ultimate betrayal to the woman who deserved his loyalty. He would only ever love Kari.

And now he was on his way to ask for the other woman's help to celebrate his son's birthday. That was what he needed to focus on. Jonah. Kari would want this day to be filled with joy for Jonah.

Gina had insisted on coming along so she could

watch the kids while he spoke with Belle. He also knew that she hated sitting around with nothing to do.

He glanced at his son. Jonah deserved his birthday to be full of smiles and all the silliness of a five-year-old. Long ago Quinn had made a promise to himself that he wouldn't let his guilt be transferred to his son, even by accident.

Before he could cut the engine, all three kids were out of their seat belts and running to the barn. He followed them. Gina walked beside him with slow, measured steps. She'd never been one to hurry.

"She might not want to help us, you know." He stuffed his hands into his pockets. "Just because she's a single mom doesn't mean she's a party planner for every kid that comes through her town."

"She's a caregiver, not just a mother to her children. You can see it in the way she cares for everyone around her. Just explain. She'll want to help. I also have faith that she will do the right thing when it comes to the land."

His mother-in-law had always been way too optimistic. By the time he and Gina entered the barn, his three had joined Belle's girls as if they were old pros at hand-feeding orphaned goats.

Lucy, Belle's youngest, ran to him. "How are the babies? Did you bring them?"

"No. They're tucked away safely in their crate. We don't want to move them around too much."

Cassie herded them all out to feed the chickens and Gina followed.

A tractor stood nearby, its hood open. Belle was working on it. She tossed a rag to the side, picked up a wrench and went back to work.

"You need any help?"

She stood, shaking her head as she made eye contact. Her long braid fell down the center of her back and, for a moment, he wanted to unbraid it and see what it looked like free.

"I need a new tractor, but that's not gonna happen anytime soon. You don't know anything about carburetors, do you?"

That brought him back to the present. He wasn't sure he'd even recognize one. "My offer to help was more like 'Is there someone I can call for you?'"

She laughed. "On a ranch, you take care of things yourself. There's no calling."

At the sound of her laughter, his skin tightened, and he leaned closer to her. He scowled at his reaction. Going to the other side of the tractor, he put distance between them. "How long have you been running this place?"

Hands on her hips, she glared at the engine. "Feels like my whole life. I left for a little bit, trying to save a marriage that wasn't worth saving. My uncle needed me here. The boys had all left him—or he'd kicked them out, depending on who you talk to. He wasn't doing well, so I stepped in to make sure the ranch kept running."

"I'm still a bit confused as to who owns the ranch and how you're all related."

She laughed as she wiped a wrench. "So are we. Technically Xavier, Damian and their little sister, Gabby, own the majority. My mom owns some, but she's missing. I've managed the ranch for several years now."

"You had to be awful young when Cassie was born."

She shifted to the side, looking uncomfortable. "Yeah. I was sixteen."

Okay, that surprised him. Sixteen. "Wow."

Her gaze dropped, but her jaw tightened. He was getting too personal. "Sorry. That wasn't the reason I wanted to speak to you, anyway. I have something to ask you."

Her shoulders relaxed, and she rolled her neck. With a slight curve to her lips, she looked at him. "What can I help you with?"

"Jonah is turning five this weekend. I know there's not much time, but five is a big deal and I want him to have a good time, but I have no idea what to do. Since you're from here, I thought you might have an idea or know kids we can invite to his birthday party. With his mother gone, I'm not good at this kind of thing, but he's getting older and it was the day we lost her, so…" *Stop talking now.* "I want him to have good memories. Could you help us?"

Her brilliant eyes went soft. "Oh. Did she die giving birth?" She wrinkled her nose. "Sorry, not my business."

"It's okay. It was almost five years ago. We were traveling in South America. Jonah doesn't have any memories of her. I tend to struggle with the day because we lost her, but I want him to feel special on his birthday. He'll remember this one. I need more than just a cake and a song. I don't know what to do. Kari, my wife, always planned the girls' parties." He pressed his lips together to stop talking.

Her eyes went wide, and he saw her making the connections. "Oh. I'm so sorry." She reached forward and placed a hand on his arm. "I can help. I happen to personally know someone who owns a pirate ship that is perfect for a five-year-old's birthday. My brother, Elijah. I can ask him. If they're booked, they have a private party room upstairs at the Painted Dolphin. It overlooks the Gulf. If not, we can do something here on the ranch. We have a long strip of beach and horses. We can make sure he has the best memories for his birthday."

"A pirate ship? Wow." He chuckled. "That sounds like something Kari would have loved. My kids, too. They love reading adventure stories and have scary crazy imaginations. Gina told me you'd have the connections." He leaned closer and whispered, "Once again, she was right. Let's not tell her, okay?"

"I wondered why your mother-in-law was staying with you. She must be a great help."

"Kari was an only child, so Gina has been with us ever since Jonah was born."

He stopped. She'd been with Kari when the girls were born. Had traveled with them most of the time. But not that trip. Did she feel as guilty as he did? He shook his head. He'd have to talk to her later. "I don't know what I would have done without her. All the traveling for my job can make it necessary to have a fulltime caregiver."

"Being a single parent makes any job even harder." She tossed another tool back into the box.

"You seem to have good family support. Does your ex help with the kids, too?" He wanted to pull the question back as he was asking it. It was too personal.

"No. He moved out of state. There were issues, but he never was involved with the girls, even when we were married. The ranch is hard work but is a great place for my girls. The only home we've even known.

We all want a place we're connected to. I wanted this to be a safe harbor for my family. Xavier, Damian and Elijah have each had their issues and Frank had chased them away. They needed a place to heal."

The happy voices of their children stopped the questions he wanted to ask. Elijah approached, following the small herd of little people. They were telling him about the ocelot kittens.

This was a good interruption. They were getting more personal than Quinn was comfortable with. He wanted to dig for more information about her, not just about the ranch. Not good.

The woman standing in front of him intrigued him in ways he didn't like.

Chapter Five

Belle dropped her shoulders and went to work on the old engine. Elijah's appearance was a relief. The tension in her muscles eased. She had gotten too personal too fast. She needed space from Quinn. He was the kind of man who made it hard to think clearly.

The way he treated his children and mother-in-law—at least in public—was too good to believe. She needed to be careful and not get pulled in, only to find out the truth too late. Men were good at hiding secrets.

Elijah patted her shoulder. "Got a call that the northwest fence is down. If that's true, your bull could be in Jacoby's pasture."

That cut off all wayward thoughts of the new man living on her ranch. "He'd like that. Who called, and why did they call you?" Everyone knew she ran the daily operations on the Diamondback.

He shrugged. "They left a message, and it was a number I didn't know."

"That doesn't make any sense. We checked all the fences yesterday after the storm. There were a couple of damaged areas, but we patched them."

"We might want to check to see if it's been cut. That bull is valuable, and Jacoby might not mind some new blood in his herd. I'll ride out with you. Let's call a few of the guys in. If the herd crossed the fence, it might be a bigger job."

"I can help," Quinn offered.

Elijah scanned him with a critical eye. "No offense, but handling bulls and dealing with fences can be hard work, and if you don't know what you're doing, it can create more problems."

Quinn nodded and gave him an easy smile. "My mom was a top-tier equestrian. I grew up in some big arenas in Houston. Mind you, it was dressage and hunters, but I can sit any horse. Having the wrong people in the field can cause more work. Did a job on a little place not far from here." He gestured to the north. "You might have heard of it. The King Ranch." He grinned. "Do you do the work from horses or ATVs?"

Hunters and dressage? Those were not the usual cowboy hobbies. Then he threw in the King Ranch. She narrowed her gaze at him.

"*The* King Ranch?"

He nodded.

Everything she learned about him only intrigued her more. "We're on horses." It wouldn't be easy for her or her resolve to remain uninterested if she saw him in the saddle. She refocused her attention. The kids had goats climbing on them... "Are y'all ready for breakfast? Your *tío* Elijah and I have to ride out."

"Yes!" all five yelled as one. She laughed.

"Y'all act as if you're starving. The sun is just peeking over the horizon." She headed to the house, her group of egg wranglers trailing behind. She looked over her shoulder. Elijah and Quinn were behind the kids, deep in conversation. They were plotting, she knew it.

Jazz and Rosie were already in the kitchen. Jazz had the egg casserole out of the oven and was warming the tortillas.

"Thanks, Jazz."

"No problem. Elijah said it might be an all-day job. I'll take the girls to school."

At times Belle felt so alone, but she wasn't. She hugged Jazz. She had taken her family for granted. "I'm so grateful for everything you do for us."

Her sister-in-law stiffened in surprise, then squeezed her tight. "We love you."

Belle squeezed her again. She didn't show affection often enough.

Cassie, Lucy and Rosie grabbed glasses, plates and orange juice without being told. The men entered the kitchen. "Quinn, thank you for your offer, but I'm sure you have tons to do after the fire." Ranch work sounded romantic, but it was hard and dirty. Her ex-husband, Jared, and her uncle had avoided it whenever they could. Even Elijah and Xavier preferred to be out in their boats. But they were loyal and did what was needed.

Gina came into the kitchen. "I can do whatever needs to be done. Quinn can help you. He's good with horses and is a hard worker."

"Gina." Quinn sounded embarrassed. Great. They had another matchmaker.

Belle glanced at the people gathered in her kitchen. In a very short time, Quinn and his family had slipped right into their circle.

"We have it taken care of. Jazz takes the girls to school, and Elijah and I will ride out to the fences."

"I want to go to school!" Jonah yelled, louder than necessary.

"We do, too," the twins said as one.

Gina moved the basket of tortillas on the table. "I'll take the kids to feed the ocelots. Then we have some shopping to do. After that we'll visit the school and get information. They think it'll be all fun and games with their friends, but school is work, too. Just like the work I give them."

"But with friends," Hannah said quietly.

Elijah poured orange juice for the kids as they sat. "That sounds good. It's an amazing school," he said. "It'll be great for Quinn to join us. We won't have to call anyone else, and we can head out now. If he knows what he's doing, it'll make things go faster."

She avoided looking at Quinn. The more she was around him, the more she liked him. Nothing good would come out of that. Pulling tortillas out of the basket, Belle made breakfast tacos. "Okay. Then wrap up some tacos, get some coffee and let's head out. There's enough light to see where we're going. Jazz, thank you for coming so early." She gave her girls a hard "mother stare." "You will be good listeners and not ask for any favors or treats. Straight to school. Understood?"

They both nodded. "Yes, ma'am."

Filling her water container, she headed to the door. The men walked in silence on either side of her as they headed to the barns. Once they were on the horses, Elijah could take Quinn with him. She didn't have to entertain him. Being a widower and a single dad didn't make him a good guy.

She had her own scars from men who had vowed to protect her. That wasn't fair. Xavier had intervened when Jared had lost control, and Elijah had saved her more than once from their uncle's rage.

But then again, they had left her alone to handle the ranch more than once.

Did Quinn's smooth charm and good looks hide a darker side? She glanced at him. Or was he as open and honest as he seemed?

The leather creaked as Quinn relaxed into the rhythm of the horse. It had been a long time since he'd been in the saddle. He loved the coastal bend with its endless skies and soft horizons. There was a storm over the Gulf, so the weather was moody.

Damian had met them at the barn with the horses ready. Which was impressive, since the man had only one arm. He'd mounted in a smooth motion and ridden out without saying a word. Belle rode with him.

As they left the barn, Elijah came up next to him. "I'll head into the Jacoby property with Damian to look for the bull. You and Belle tend to the fence. Nothing fancy, just enough to keep our stock on our side."

"Sounds good. He didn't look happy about me joining you today." He nodded to Damian. "Does he work on the ranch?"

"When the mood strikes him. He has the cabin farthest out and works with the horses. He returned from the Middle East about three years ago. Lost part of an arm and leg, and the ability to interact with people, so don't let him bother you. He's a good man."

Quinn narrowed his eyes and studied the man. There was no evidence he was missing a leg.

"As long as you don't mess with his family or animals, he'll leave you alone. He's been a huge help to Belle."

Belle. His brain wouldn't let go of her comment about having her daughter at sixteen and her hints of an abusive husband and uncle. Then there was that scar on her temple. She touched it more than she was probably aware of.

He wanted to know everything about her.

As if reading his thoughts, Belle joined him on his other side. "This is perfect timing."

"What?" He cleared his throat and studied his hands.

She smiled and pointed to her brother. "Elijah is the one with the pirate ship."

Relief caused him to chuckle. "Now, that's something you don't expect to hear when you're out working cattle."

Elijah laughed. "I'll agree to that. Do you have a need for a pirate ship?"

Belle shifted in her saddle. "His son is about to turn five. Since they're new in town, he doesn't know anyone or anywhere to hold a party. They want to make a splash. Pun intended."

Elijah groaned. "Stop." He looked at Quinn. "When is this party?"

"Next week. His birthday is on a Saturday this year." The tension was back in his shoulders, and he locked his gaze on the horizon.

Elijah nodded. "As soon as I return, I'll have Selena look into the date. She runs the office and keeps us all organized. Does it matter what time? If we're booked, maybe we can run a private launch."

"That would be great. Whatever works for you." The De La Rosas had taken him and his family in, helping him however they could. They had no idea why he was even in town. The guilt that settled in his gut didn't feel right. The sooner he could tell them, the better.

Belle grinned and tipped her hat. "My work here is done. I'm going to ride ahead." With one click, she galloped off.

"So, you and Belle do the work at the Diamondback, but your cousins are the owners. Damian is a cousin." The family dynamics were a little confusing. Who would he need on his side when he made his move?

"He's Xavier's younger brother. But we were raised together by my uncle, so we're more like siblings. Belle gets all the credit for running the ranch and keeping it working. We've each abandoned her one way or another. I was completely checked out for a while. My uncle and I had some major issues, and we couldn't be within a mile of each other without coming to blows."

"But he and Belle got along?"

"Oh, no. But he didn't knock her around like he did us boys. He was still verbally abusive, which was one of the reasons I wanted to do more than yell at him. She's tough, and she stood her ground, but I guess she learned that the hard way. She's so determined to save the ranch for her family. We never quite understood. If you asked any of us guys, we'd sell on a dime. She's done so much and is turning it around. We've been working together, and she has some great ideas that could not only benefit Diamondback Ranch, but bring more business to Port Del Mar. The best thing that happened to her was that loser of a husband finally leaving."

Belle moved naturally with her horse, swaying with each easy step. The vast landscape around them blurred at the edges of his eyesight. His attention was held hostage.

She belonged here, on the land. He wanted to know more about the husband, but that would make it too obvious that he was interested. And he wasn't—or shouldn't be, anyway. "What kind of ideas?" He needed to keep it professional. Maybe it would all work out, and they could share the same goal.

"The majority of the working ranch is inland from the coast. So, if she sold the two hundred acres that runs along the shoreline, she could use the money to restore the rest and keep the ranch solid."

Unease slipped along his spine. "So y'all plan to sell your strip of beach?"

"We're looking into it. We've had people out to evaluate the land and see if it could be developed."

If Quinn's mission was successful, they wouldn't be able to develop along the coastline. Dropping the value. It would become worthless on a commercial level, but priceless for the wildlife that needed open land and beaches.

Personal relationships were a hassle and got in the way of his objectives. He had one job. Preserve the coastline. Then move on to the next location.

Belle waved to them. She had dismounted and was unloading supplies from a saddlebag. The fence was down. The wire tangled in a muddy mess of hoofprints left no question that her stock had moved into the other pasture. Damian was already searching.

Elijah guided his horse along the tracks the cattle had left behind. "I'll see how far they moved in and how many. Hopefully, Damian and I can get them back without an issue."

As they rode off, Belle was already untangling the fence. Quinn stood silent for a while, but she didn't seem to remember he was there. "What do you need me to do?"

She glanced at him, then held up the end of a barbed-wire strand. "Can you find the other end of this?"

Taking a few steps to the side, he dug around in the mud that had been disturbed by what looked to be a small stampede. "Here it is." He lifted it for her inspection.

With a tilt of her head, she narrowed her eyes. "You're a scientist. What do you see?"

At first, he thought she was being flippant, but a glance at the wire told him something was off. The cut was too clean to be a random break. He looked closer, then studied the second strand. "They've been cut."

She sighed. "Yeah. That's what I thought, too."

"If your neighbor was looking to borrow your bull, there have to be better ways of doing it."

She stared over the pasture next to hers. "Yeah. Jacoby can be grumpy and stingy. If the cattle happen to push the fence down during a storm, it's a no-fault situation. Then if my bull happens to spend some time hanging out with his herd before we find him and bring him home, he would take advantage of the situation. No harm done." She shook her head. "But he wouldn't do this."

He helped her reset the post and untangle the wire.

"I'll need heavier equipment and more supplies to fix it properly," she continued. "We'll make a temporary fix for now." Crimping tool in hand, she made a loop at the end of the broken strand. Her hands were fast and steady.

"You're good at this."

"For a girl?" She glared at him from her half-bent position, then snorted. "I learned long ago I had to do twice as much to be considered half as good as my brother and cousins."

"*Girl* is not a word that comes to mind when I watch you work." He leaned on the post they had reset and tilted his head as he watched her. "My wife was very hands-on. She didn't back down, no matter how big the job was. She didn't just sit on the board of the Foundation. She worked in the field." He grinned, remembering how frustrated she would get when her size would get in the way of what she wanted. She would have liked Belle.

Belle straightened, surprise shining in her eyes. "Looking at your mother-in-law and daughters, I would say your wife was very petite."

"Really? The size of a person equals their abilities?" She blushed.

"You've heard that old cliché that dynamite comes in small packages? Kari was a tiny bundle of dynamite, and when she got going, there was no stopping her. She ran the Foundation and she worked in the most remote locations. Once she had a mission in her sights, nothing held her back."

"You were okay with that? Her running the show?"

And just like that, his good mood was gone. He had been okay with it—until it had gotten her killed. He should have been stronger. If… He took a deep breath and turned away from Belle. He wanted to remember his wife without guilt.

He shouldn't be sharing this much about his wife with another woman.

Tall coastal grass waved in the breeze. In the distance, Elijah and Damian were heading their way. Good timing. He pointed to the field. "Looks like they were partially successful."

A huge, dark red bull plodded between them, his head down, his hooves dragging. "They found your bull, but those aren't your cows, are they?" A small group of solid black heifers followed them like a pack of sad puppies. "I've only seen Brahman cows on your place."

Belle arched her back, then twisted to the side to follow his gaze. A low guttural sound came from her. "The Angus cows belong to Jacoby. What happened? Charming doesn't look good at all." A scowl wrinkled her face, and she put her hands on her hips.

"Where are my heifers?" She raised her voice so they could hear her. As they drew closer, cuts and abrasions were visible all over Charming's hide.

Elijah rode to meet them. Damian pulled his horse up and waited at the bull's side. Not being coaxed along, Charming stopped and nosed the grass. The nervous cows bunched together, glaring suspiciously at them.

Elijah stood in his saddle, then looked over his shoulder at the bull. "We found him in a ravine with these cows."

Turning to them, he leaned across his saddle horn and crossed his arms. The grim expression on his face warned them it would not be a happy story. "The edge of the ravine looked as if it had fallen out from under them. They couldn't get back out. That might have saved them from being stolen. First, the trail led us to truck marks, a big eighteen-wheeler-type truck and trailer with a bunch of hoofprints disappearing right into it. The only reason Charming wasn't taken was that he and a few of Jacoby's girls had fallen into the ravine.

The bawling was how we found them. They were out of water and grass."

"So, Jacoby stole his own cattle and a handful of ours?" Belle looked at the coiled wire. "He wouldn't do that. So who? Our herd is just building up."

Her jaw was tight, and for a moment she looked lost and scared. If they stood here much longer, Quinn thought she might cry. That upset him much more than it should have. He wanted to help but wasn't even sure what to say.

He pulled out his phone. "I'll call Sheriff Cantu. You call Jacoby. Let him know what's going on. Maybe it's a misunderstanding."

She stiffened. Elijah and Damian both raised their eyebrows. His gaze darted between them. "What?"

She waved to Damian and Elijah to move the big bull over the property line. "Elijah, call Jacoby. He'll be less defensive than if I call. I'll report the incident to Cantu." Then she focused her full attention on Quinn. "Thank you for your help, but this is a family matter, and we'll take care of it. Your help is no longer needed."

And with that, she turned her back to him, putting him firmly in his place.

Anger seethed under her skin, making it tight. She let her guard down and what happened? Her cattle were stolen, and Quinn stepped in to make her decisions. With the bull on the correct side of the fence, she yanked the wire harder than necessary.

"Do you need me to help with that?" he offered.

Just a few minutes ago she was enjoying his company. She gave him her hardest glare. Did he think her weak? She'd never need a man to help her again. She didn't.

Without a word, she went to work. Her hand was sore, her thighs numb and her skin raw under the thick leather gloves.

Life had given her much worse to handle. She wasn't going to give him the satisfaction that she couldn't do the job.

Elijah had Jacoby on the phone. Hanging up, he waved goodbye to Belle as he and Damian herded Charming to the smaller pasture to the south. It was closer to the barns.

Quinn was messing with the scrap wire. He was lingering because he didn't think she could handle this by herself. Her jaw was so tight it hurt. "I know my way to the barns. You don't have to stick around on my account. I'm a big girl, if you hadn't noticed."

He eyed her in a way that said he wasn't going to touch that with a ten-foot pole.

"I'm not staying because you need any assistance. It isn't smart for anyone to be out here alone. Especially now that it looks as if there are criminal elements involved. I'd stay if it was Elijah or Damian." He adjusted his hat. "I didn't mean to offend you. This is a stressful situation. Someone is stealing from you. You have every right to be angry. I was trying to help."

As she pulled the last strand, her fingers slipped, and the wire popped free. Coiling back, it whipped past her, bouncing off her arm when she covered her face. Losing her balance, she fell backward into the mud. She wanted to yell and cry but bit down hard instead.

"Belle." His voice was low and soft. Balanced on his heels, he was eye level with her. "Were you hit?"

Her fist clenched in the mud. She was proud of herself for not throwing a mudball at the gorgeous man who had done nothing wrong but enter her world when she was falling apart.

She wiped her face and checked her arm. "No, just embarrassed." If the ground wanted to open and swallow her right this minute, she'd be fine with that.

He slipped his work glove off and held out his hand, waiting for her to take it. If she didn't accept his offer of help now, she'd be acting the brat. It might be too late for that, anyway, so she shouldn't make it worse. Her poor glove was coated in mud. Using her left hand, she pulled it off and put her hand in his.

His big hand engulfed hers. She'd never been dainty, but he made her feel small. She shouldn't like it.

Warmth zipped through her from his touch. "Thank you." Avoiding his gaze, she tried to clean off her jeans.

"I'm sorry I overstepped. I've been running the Foundation alone for almost five years now, and making quick decisions is what everyone expects of me. No excuse. This is your operation, and I shouldn't have barked orders."

Her gaze darted across her boot toes. Did he mean his words, or was it a trap? She raised her chin until she was meeting his gaze. "I appreciate that." She glanced at the horses grazing close by. "I might have overreacted."

If Elijah were within earshot, he'd be doubled over laughing. He always said she was the queen of understatements with a dash of drama. Quinn's smile was tentative but real, not flashy or cocky. And she truly appreciated that, more than he'd understand if she tried to explain.

The wire was coiled around the post. One brow

arched high, he waited for her to say something. With a sigh, she shook her head and chuckled. "Would you help me close the gap between the posts? It seems to be a two-person job."

He was polite enough not to laugh, allowing her to keep her dignity. Oh, if she was honest with herself, she liked him, liked him on a very dangerous level.

Wire in hand, he grinned at her. "What next?"

That was the question, wasn't it?

Chapter Six

The sun wasn't up yet, but today he'd been out of bed before the kids. He didn't want to give too much thought as to why he was ready to get the day started, or he'd fall into a bad mood. The last time this kind of lightness took over, he'd been pursuing his wife. She'd been the love of his life. His whole life.

How could he even imagine kissing another woman?

He had promised to love Kari forever.

He'd never broken a promise to her, and he wasn't going to now.

The warmth of the coffee cup didn't help. How had kissing Belle even seeped into his brain?

"Daddy, Cassie says it's not fair we get to keep the baby ocelots." Meg walked into the little kitchen area.

Hannah was right behind her, arms crossed. "They were the ones that found them, and it was on their ranch. She said we should have joint custody. Why can't we?"

Forcing his mind to concentrate on his children, he took a sip of bitter coffee. They should always be forefront in his thoughts. "It's complicated."

"Like a dating status?" The girls giggled.

He frowned as he glanced up. What did they know about social media statuses? This needed further investigation. They didn't have phones, and he limited their use of the internet, so they shouldn't know any of that stuff.

He glanced at Gina. She had her back to them, preparing breakfast.

"Cassie and Lucy's mom is single, like you." Hannah leaned toward him. "Both of you have kids. You should go on a date."

"Yes!" Meg gave him a cheeky smile. "A movie and dinner, then dancing. That's what grown-ups do on a date. Why don't you date?"

The change in topic had his brain struggling to stay in the conversation. He slid into a chair at the table and gathered his thoughts.

After talking over each other, they went quiet and stared at him. Sweat ran down his spine. "It's…" There was no way he could use the word *complicated* again, but it was the truth. If he couldn't muddle through his own feelings and thoughts, how did he explain it to two nine-year-olds?

He was saved as Jonah dragged himself into the room, and Gina placed a bowl of eggs and avocado over rice in front of each of them.

"What I need from you is a list of activities that would be fun for Jonah's birthday. It's going to be here soon, and the De La Rosa family is letting us go out on their pirate ship."

The kids screamed and cheered. Jonah stood in his chair. "Really? I get a whole ship for my birthday?" His face glowed with excitement. "This is the best birthday ever!"

"Yes, sir. Sit before you fall. Let me know some of the stuff you want so I can give a list to Ms. Belle."

Gina smiled at him and patted his arm. The girls started listing idea after idea. Finished eating, he stood. "Baba will be taking you to the ranch this morning. I need to get an early start to some research." He kissed each of them, then headed out to the barns. Elijah had given him permission to explore the ranch with a horse.

His team had already gathered pages of data, but he needed actual hands-on evidence to pull it all together. Maybe he wouldn't even find proof of what he suspected.

As he rode the horse along the rise, miles of shoreline met the ocean. It would be like searching for a single grain of rice in the Gulf, but his instincts told him this private bit of beach was hiding several treasures. The spring breeze and rising sun slowed his thoughts. On the ranch, he was communicating with God in a way he hadn't in years.

Scanning the beach, he pulled up the horse and focused on the marks in the sand. Heart pumping fast, he dismounted and eased closer.

Turtle tracks.

Leaving the horse to graze nearby, he climbed the sand dunes. Easing his way through the tall grass, he spotted a Kemp's ridley female laying eggs in the sand.

Tablet in hand, he recorded the site, then logged in date, location, weather and all the other details that might help them tell a story. He'd need to report it also.

Looking for more tracks, he moved north.

He walked with the reins in hand. Nests could be well hidden, and he didn't want to miss anything. Soon he found evidence of another nest. Blood rushed through his body. More tracks, at least ten females.

The quietness was broken by the sound of small engines.

Leaving the beach, he climbed the dunes as Belle and Xavier came into view. They each had a couple of men with them on the ATVs. Men who didn't have the look of ranch hands. One sported a cowboy hat and fancy boots, the kind for show. Too much money spent on them to wear for dirty work.

The other three men were all business. His gut burned. Belle was showing the land to potential developers.

They stopped, and she introduced him to the strangers. One was a Realtor. Protectiveness swamped him as he stood between these men and the nesting females.

A bit of small chitchat, and then they were moving on to look at the rest of the land. "Belle, I need to talk with you."

She frowned, then looked at Xavier. "Warren, you wanted to drive. You can follow Xavier to see the rest. Swing by on your way back to pick me up."

With a nod, they were gone. He glanced to the edge of the dunes. If the turtles were nervous, they wouldn't be able to lay their eggs.

"What is it, Quinn? You seem upset. Is everything okay?"

"There are Kemp's ridley sea turtles nesting on your beach."

"Oh. Um." She turned to the Gulf, her well-worn cowboy hat shading her face. "We've had them before. We just need to report the location."

"It's more than one. You might have an arribada on your ranch."

She swung back to face him, a crease between her brows. "What does that mean?"

"A large group of females return to the place they hatched to lay their eggs. The largest is in Mexico, but I predicted that we could find one in Texas." He knew this could end Belle's plans for the ranch but hesitated to say anything yet.

Heading to the dunes, she disappeared into the tall grass. Her arms flailed as she fell.

"Belle?"

The only sound was a low moan. "Belle." He went to his knees at her side. He checked her for injuries but wasn't sure what he was even looking for. "What's wrong?"

"My foot's stuck in something." She tried to sit up but then held her head. "I hit something as I fell."

He moved to her leg. Buried under the sand was an odd snare-looking thing. "Your foot is in some sort of trap that probably washed up long ago. Can you move your foot?"

"Ouch. It hurts." She pulled at it. "I can't get it out."

He took his backpack off and pulled out some tools. "I'm breaking off the metal and wood pieces. We might have to slip your foot out of your boot." He studied her eyes. "How's the head? Vision?"

"A bit blurry at first, but it's clearing. It was a shock to find myself looking at the sky. My foot just kept going. The ground was gone." She closed her eyes. "I'm okay."

"Not sure about that. We need a doctor to make that diagnosis."

"No doctor." She moaned. "No insurance."

"No worries. The clinic'll bill you."

He wasn't going to argue with her while she was pinned. "Your boot saved your foot from being impaled by the bars of the trap. I've cut them away, so now I'm going to pull your leg out. Tell me if you feel anything that shouldn't be there. I don't want your skin to be broken." He looked into her gray-green eyes. The pain was clear. "Are you ready?"

She nodded.

With his hands on her leg, he gently lifted until she was clear. Once her foot was out of the boot, she tried to stand and just about fell again.

Hooking one arm under her leg, he lifted her against his chest. He adjusted her weight, then went up the hill toward the horse. "Do you know how far out Elijah is?"

She shook her head.

"Then I'll drive you to a clinic. You need X-rays. Are you current on your tetanus shot? We're going to have to double up."

"Put me down."

"I know you're strong, but I don't think you'll get far if you try to walk." He grunted as he topped the dune.

He shifted her in his arms. The horse was close.

"I'm too heavy." She shivered and groaned. He felt the pain tightening her muscles. "You can't carry me."

He chuckled. "I'm carrying you as we speak." His arms tightened around her. The feel of her in his arms was too right.

"You're going to drop me or hurt yourself."

Her hair brushed his face. He loved her scent. "I've lifted orcas back into the ocean."

"Did you just compare me to a whale?" Her face was pressed against his chest.

He was an idiot. A middle-school boy at his first dance knew better than to compare a woman to a large animal.

There had to be something to make it better. "The most majestic creature on the planet." He let her slip to the ground as he stood next to the horse. He pressed his lips to her forehead to do a fast wellness check and placed his fingers against her pulse.

"I fell. I'm not dying."

"We'll let the doctor decide that." He draped her arm over his shoulders. "Does this horse allow a left-side mount?"

She nodded, and he helped her place her good foot in the stirrup.

Once she was settled, he swung up behind her. No woman had been so perfect in his arms other than Kari. Now he held Belle as the horse slowly plodded its way to the ranch house, and he wanted to hold her closer.

Soon she would know the whole truth and there would be no chance of a relationship between them. He would have to tell her everything before long.

By the end of summer, he would be in South America, and she would hate him.

"Izabella, wake up." A deep male voice was too close. Blood rushing through her veins, she sat up. Blinking, she felt her thoughts tumble in her brain. Why was she asleep in a car?

Quinn. He had carried her. A groan escaped.

Not many men could make her feel petite and feminine, but he had. Seriously, how did he do this to her?

At least it was just a sprain. She would be back to work in the morning. The doctor had given her some painkillers that knocked her out. Those were a no go. They wouldn't be crossing her lips again.

"How are you feeling?"

"The kids?" Her brain was so foggy.

"They're in town with Selena and Xavier. Elijah has the ranch covered."

She managed to nod. "The receipts. Give them to me." She reached for her purse. "I'll pay you back."

"It wasn't that much." He shrugged.

"I don't need charity. I've always paid my own way."

He mumbled something about stubborn people, then nodded as if he agreed. Eyes narrowed, she glared at him with suspicion. "Give me the receipts. All of them."

He ignored her and slipped out of his Land Rover. Then he reappeared at her side.

She would have insisted he hand them over right now, but she was tired, and her body ached. He unbuckled her and lifted her into his arms.

This again? His breath caressed her ear. Why was he carrying her this time? She weighed too much. She closed her eyes and melted in his arms. It wasn't fair that he was the one that made her feel safe. It must be the meds. Before she could protest, he had her on the sofa.

Nestling into the soft blankets and pillows, she rested her eyes. Those receipts would be hers soon.

Petting the sofa, she sighed. "I love you."

"What?"

"I was talking to my sofa. Quinn, you must stop carrying me around. I'm too heavy. Why…?" She tried to finish the thought, but her brain wasn't working. This was why she never took meds. She hated any type of weakness.

Her eyes closed again. Jerkily, she forced them open. There was no time for sleep.

Quinn. Twisting, she looked up and saw that he was sorting the meds the doctor had given her. He couldn't be real. And that jaw, she wanted to trace it, with her lips. Her eyes went to the little bones at the base of his neck. She didn't even know what they were called, but man, his were amazing.

How did he have her thinking about bringing a man into her life? With him, maybe…maybe she could… She sat up. Then grabbed her head.

Oh. That was too fast. Resting her head on the sofa, she looked at the ceiling for a while before closing her eyes.

Quinn might be nice and helpful now, but he wouldn't stay that way.

Showing weakness, even to her brother and cousins, put everything she had worked for in jeopardy. Arms braced on the edge of the sofa cushion, she pushed up, but then pain shot up her leg.

Strong hands held her shoulders. Quinn gently eased her deeper into her little nest.

"Do you need something? You know, it's okay to ask for help." He pointed to her Bible on the coffee table. "Even Jesus asked His disciples for help."

She laughed. "Yeah. They also disappointed Him. They argued about His purpose. They fell asleep. They denied Him in His moment of greatest need."

"Wow. Okay."

She didn't want to debate scripture. Her brain was too muddled. Eyes closed, she fell into the mound of pillows. "No more painkillers."

"Izabella." The rough whisper tickled her skin as his hand brushed her hair. "You need to let others take care of you occasionally. You can't do it all by your-self all the time."

She just needed one more minute; then she'd get up. "Quinn, thank you for your help, but I've got it."

He chuckled. "I know you do."

"I'm fine."

Leaning back, he smiled. Not the big, flashy trust-me smile, but one that said he understood. Her heart flipped. No, no, no. "You take care of everyone. Who takes care of you?"

Moving forward, he was inches from her face. She could see the ocean in his eyes as they searched her. "You're strong, but you need someone who takes care of you." His eyes dropped to her mouth.

She held her breath. She might have even moved closer to him. She was going to kiss him.

Frozen, they hung in midair. She closed the space and, just as their lips touched, the back door slammed, and they jumped apart. "Mom!"

Stupid. Stupid. Stupid. What was wrong with her? *Brain fog.* The meds.

She took a deep breath and cleared her head of nega-tive words. No one was going to make her feel less than ever again. Not even herself.

"Belle, I'm sorry. I shouldn't have done that." He stood. Moved away from her.

Good. Distance was what she needed. Lots of it. Trusting him was too risky, but apparently, she couldn't trust herself, either.

Once the meds were out of her system she would be back in the saddle and in charge.

She'd help him with Jonah's birthday party, then cut all ties to Quinn Sinclair.

Chapter Seven

"Daddy. Hannah has my tiara!" Meg screeched from behind him. His three children were in the second row. Belle's girls were in the last bench seat. He'd been given kid duty when Belle and Gina had left earlier to set up Jonah's party on the pirate ship.

It had been a crazy couple of days. The problem with the missing cattle on the ranch had her busier than usual, and he'd been buried in research and data, trying to determine their options before approaching the De La Rosas.

"I traded her my eyepatch." Hannah clung to the tiara as her sister reached across Jonah to take it off her head.

"Did not. You gave me the eyepatch."

"Stop. No fighting on my birthday." Jonah covered his ears. "No fighting."

"Meg, get into your seat and tighten your seat belt." Quinn gave them his best dad voice. "We don't have time for bickering. Hannah, you wanted to be a pirate for Jonah's birthday. So, wear your eyepatch and be happy."

After giving up her crown, Hannah huffed and

crossed her arms. "But I want to be a princess pirate. Why can't I be both?"

"You can be," Cassie added from the back.

"Not without a crown." Meg slipped the tiara on and fixed her hair.

"You picked the pirate costume. It's Jonah's birthday, and we get to be on a pirate ship. There will be a treasure. Forget the costumes and enjoy the adventure. Your mother always said that joy and jealousy could not coexist inside you," Quinn said.

"I'm not jealous!" Hannah pouted.

"What does that mean?" Lucy and Cassie asked at the same time.

Quinn frowned. He hadn't thought ahead as to how to explain something Kari had said all the time. "Jealousy. You want something someone else has, and they don't want to give it up. Hannah is upset and in a bad mood because she wants what her sister has. Which happens to us all. It's normal. But if you stay upset, you won't have any fun at the party. That's where the 'no joy' comes in. If you stay focused on what you don't have, then you miss out on the fun everyone else is having sailing on a pirate ship. Worse, because of your bad mood, no one else can have fun, either. Do you want joy or bitterness?"

Hannah nodded. "I'm sorry, Meg. And Jonah. I want everyone to have fun today."

Cassie leaned forward, hand on the seat in front of her. "Mr. Sinclair, can we call Rosie? She has tons of princess stuff, along with fishing and cowboy gear. Maybe Hannah can borrow one from her. She'll be at the party."

All five pairs of eyes looked at him in the rearview mirror.

Jonah lifted his new boots in the air. "I'm a cowboy pirate. Hannah can be a pirate princess. Can I have a cowboy hat?"

Quinn passed his phone to Hannah. "Sounds like a plan. But if she says no, we are all good with that, too. Be nice."

"Yes, sir." They all smiled. He savored the moment. Most of the time, he doubted his parenting skills. Kari had always seemed to know the right answer, and as the girls got older, he knew they would miss her even more. For now, he was going to enjoy the win of watching his children work together instead of fight.

The dock came into view, and he sat lighter in his seat. Belle would be here. She and Gina had left earlier to gather the last-minute party supplies, pick up the cake and set up.

He'd missed her. Her ex had to be a raging idiot. How could a man walk away from her and those two girls?

He'd give anything to have his wife back; not just for himself, but for their children. Kari had made an impact on the world.

Belle was strong, compassionate, and gave to other people without thought to herself. Really, how did a man have that kind of woman as a partner and mother to his children and leave? Worse, leave her with scars? That wasn't love. Did she understand that? The urge to find the guy and knock sense into him burned at his gut.

But Belle wasn't his to protect. As much as he admired her and... He sighed and switched gears on that thought. He couldn't go there.

There shouldn't be any thought of her in his head. He'd almost kissed her.

He hadn't kissed another woman since the day he'd met Kari in the library. That was supposed to be his last first kiss. She had been his forever girl, so how could he even be thinking of Belle this way?

He needed to stay focused on the mission of their foundation. And there it was—another reason that becoming emotionally entangled with Belle was a bad idea.

It was time to tell her why he was in Port Del Mar. He'd gathered enough information and was ready to move forward. She wasn't going to like it, but he had to be up-front with her. She had people looking at the place. He couldn't avoid the conversation any longer.

"She said she already has several, so I can pick one." Hannah handed him his phone.

How had he missed the whole conversation? Belle was not good for him or his focus. The excitement in the car was tangible.

"We're here," Cassie announced, and they all cheered as he maneuvered into a parking spot close to the pier. At the end of the dock was a ship with a tall mast.

The kids climbed out one by one.

Jonah stood still. "Is this really for me?" He looked at Quinn.

An unexpected knot had formed in Quinn's throat. "Yeah, buddy." He had to grit his teeth to control the burn in his eyes. He should have been prepared. With a hard swallow, he nodded and rubbed his son's hair. "This is a special day. It's the day you joined our family, and we want to celebrate big. What better way than a pirate ship?"

Gina had been right. He had to make a shift in his mind. This could no longer be the day they lost Kari. Jonah deserved for it to be the day they gained him. Kari would want that. He had all the other days to grieve her. Their anniversary, her birthday. "It's your day, Jonah."

Meg hugged him. "Mama loved going out on boats. She would think this was the coolest."

His eyes stung. "Yes, she did."

Cassie took Jonah's hand. "This is going to be so much fun! I'll show y'all around."

All five rushed ahead. Quinn followed. Cassie was so much like her mom. Taking care of others and making sure everyone was included.

A heavy hand landed on his shoulder. "Hey, Quinn. I haven't had a chance to thank you for getting my stubborn sister to the clinic."

"Not a problem. Glad I could help. And you've done more for my family by providing the ship for Jonah's birthday party. We've never done anything this big. It's going to set high expectations."

"Belle told me how hard the day is for you, but your little man is going to have a good time, I promise. Carlos and the crew always put on the best show."

"I can't tell you how much I appreciate it. We've always been on the move with my job, and the kids haven't spent more than a year in the same town. This means a great deal."

"Childhood memories shape us as adults." Elijah wasn't looking at him, but at the faux pirate boat swaying in the water. "Jazz says I bought this ship as a redo of my own childhood. She's probably right. She usually is."

Up ahead, Belle was helping the kids board the ship. She waved at them. Elijah stopped. "Speaking of not-so-stellar childhoods, Belle was on the same ride as me. Our uncle, well…he didn't provide the most supportive home environment. Saying my sister's life has not been easy would be an understatement. Our mother was worse but then dumped us. We don't even know who our fathers are. Then there was her husband." His jaw flexed. "She protected him longer than he deserved. Strength is at her very core, but don't make the mistake of thinking she won't break."

"I'm not sure where you're going with this, but there's nothing between your sister and me. We're two single parents helping each other out."

Elijah raised both eyebrows. Quinn looked to the water. What had the other man seen that would make him doubt that statement? "I have a great deal of respect for your sister, but she's made it clear she's not interested. I'm in town long enough to get my job done. Then I'm moving on. I—" Why was he even defending himself? "Don't worry about your sister. She can take care of herself."

"I won't ever stop worrying about her. So, how long will you be in town?"

"Somewhere between three to six months."

"She knows you're leaving?"

"Yes. We haven't discussed the details, but like I said, there's nothing between us. No need for us to talk about it."

Another skeptical look, then Elijah turned and followed the kids. "Then come along, matey, and let's get this adventure underway."

A slight breeze touched his face. Tilting his head to

the sky, Quinn watched as the clouds moved and re-formed. How long was he going to keep moving the kids from town to town? The girls had already started talking about the friends in Port Del Mar they didn't want to leave.

He remembered his fifth birthday, and he wanted his son to have good memories. Memories they could use to build a new future.

Was that the reason kissing Belle and spending more time with her was in his head? It was time to move on with life?

Denial roared. He wasn't ready to let go of Kari. He would always be her husband. He didn't want another woman in his thoughts, in his kids' lives. Not that it mattered. Once he told Belle the truth, there was no future for them.

No matter how it played out, for one of them to get their way, the other was going to have to lose. A relationship would never survive that kind of conflict.

A new stuffed horse, Buck II, tucked under his arm, Quinn followed Elijah to the boat. It had taken a while for him to track one down, but it was the last gift Kari had given Jonah, and he wasn't ready to leave her behind.

Belle held the last cupcake. Should she? Should she not?

"Come on," she whispered to the sweet treat. "All the kids are gone and there's one Jolly Roger left alone. Abandoned. It's clear that you were meant for me, right?" She hadn't had any sweets all day and it was all about moderation. And if she didn't eat it, it would go to waste.

A hand landed on her shoulder and she gave a sharp scream. The cleanup crew stopped and looked at her. Heat rushed into her neck and face. She had been caught deep in conversation with a jelly-filled cupcake.

Quinn's hearty laughter didn't ease her embarrassment. He held his hands up, palms out, as if to prove he was harmless. "Belle, I'm sorry. I didn't mean to scare you."

But would he judge her? Let her know that she was way past the age of eating birthday cake? She closed her eyes. Frank's and Jared's opinions didn't matter. Even if it meant the cake would go straight to her hips.

Lowering the cupcake, she grinned at her own ridiculousness. It didn't matter what he thought about her eating habits or her hips, either. "You didn't scare me." She shrugged. "It was just a guilty conscience."

"Guilty? You don't have anything to feel guilty about. I'm in your debt." He placed his hand over his heart and bowed. "This was so much better than anything I could've come up with. Than anything that we've ever done before. And you're still here cleaning up. I can't believe Jazmine and Selena volunteered to take all the kids to the ranch." He lifted his box of party leftovers. "It might not be the right thing to say, but cleaning up is so much easier without the kids' help."

"You are so right. Jazz and Selena are awesome like that. Selena would have twelve kids if she could." She glanced at the little dessert with longing. She had vowed never to allow a man to make her feel bad about herself, and yet here she was, self-conscious about eating a cupcake in front of him. He probably wouldn't even notice.

She lifted the tiny cake and pulled at the paper lining. "I can't take all the credit. I mean, my brother does own the pirate ship. He makes it pretty easy to have spectacular birthday parties."

Quinn pointed to the red-and-black cupcake. "Are you gonna eat that or talk to it?"

Why was she holding herself back just because he was here? "We were having a meaningful conversation."

He leaned against the mast and crossed his arms over his chest. "Really? So, what kind of philosophical conversations does one have with a miniature pirate cake?"

"It's all about being the last cupcake standing. Has he been able to fulfill his purpose in life? How did it feel to watch his fellow pirates walk the plank one at a time, leaving him to stand guard alone? What kind of life is waiting for the cupcake that gets dumped in the trash? A life unfulfilled. It's so sad."

Quinn put on an exaggerated expression of mock horror. "His glorious adventure will end in a garbage bag filled with crumpled plastic cups, used napkins and discarded paper plates! No good cupcake should ever end up in the trash." He leaned toward her, a serious expression holding his lips tight and his eyes narrowed. He took the cupcake from her and held it up for their inspection. "What was your limit today? I had three. If I take one more bite, I'll explode like the old cannon. It's left to you to fulfill his destiny."

She had to laugh at his silliness. It was so refreshing not being worried about what someone thought of her. His smile alone lightened her stupid, negative self-talk. He started peeling away the rest of the paper. "I confessed to eating three. How many did you eat?"

"None."

He paused and stared at her, one eyebrow raised. "Why are we even having this discussion?"

"My uncle's favorite saying was 'A moment on the lips, forever on the hips.'" She tapped her hip. "My ex... well, it doesn't matter what he said."

He lowered his chin. "Seriously? Let me guess. Your uncle didn't give a minute's thought to his hips or gut or whatever body part he was criticizing on others. Why do you allow him to still have power over you? And your ex is a quitter who shouldn't own a minute of your thoughts."

Her throat tightened. It was the exact same thing she told herself all the time. Why did it mean more coming from him? She didn't need a man to make her feel better about herself.

She took a deep breath. It was humiliating that he saw the things she hid from everyone, including herself.

Taking the cupcake, she gave Quinn her best smile. "Hey, you're the one who compared me to an orca."

He groaned. "I will never live that down. In no shape or form was your body ever linked with the orca. Other than being loyal and agile. I was trying to impress you with my manliness and strength. I admit it was not my finest hour. But in all fairness, I have not flirted with a woman for over ten years. Tell me it didn't completely ruin any chance I have of asking you on a date."

She froze, her mouth poised to bite into the cupcake. Had he been flirting with her? There was no way he had just asked her out. He was joking.

Blinking, she bit into the cake and swallowed. The sugar flooded her taste buds in glorious sweetness as her heart did a double beat.

He was so far out of her reach, and nice, too. He was a nice guy. Her eyes went to him to see if what she'd thought she heard was correct, but he had turned his back to her.

Was he ignoring her or just moving on to the next thing on their to-do list? The words had no earth-shattering meaning to him. It was no big deal. She needed to treat it as such, too.

He moved around, gathering the last of the party favors. As they said goodbye to the crew, he slipped a solid tip their way.

He wasn't the type of man who flirted with her. And she had always been sure to cut it off before it began.

But the other day he had almost kissed her. Maybe.

She'd been kind of out of her head. She could have imagined everything. None of it meant anything. People flirted all the time. Men and women kissed. No big deal.

But it was a huge deal for her. She understood that, nowadays, it wasn't special. Which made her sad. Kissing should mean something between two people. There was nothing wrong with being old-fashioned.

She pursed her lips. If she was honest with herself, it might have more to do with fear.

What if he was playing the field? He was in town for a few months and she was close by. But he had said… She shook her head and picked up her purse. Believing anything a man said to her was the first step toward disaster. She couldn't trust him.

But she liked Quinn Sinclair. Not only was he a good father, he was a loyal son-in-law and took care of the people in his life. Maybe he was the good man he appeared to be.

She needed to be real. Her life was far from some sweet romance novel.

He turned to her. "Ready? I told Jazz and Selena I'd take you home."

At his car, he opened the door for her and, with a wink, closed it. She watched him cross in front of his car. Every woman in town had probably had a wink from him. It was like a nervous tic. They were friends. Single parents who understood the realities of life. Nothing more.

If that was the case, it wouldn't hurt to ask him out on a date, right? All through high school she had been with Jared, then had married him and had Cassie before she could finish school. She'd never gone to college, so she didn't have that experience. Never once in her life had she been on a normal date.

From the corner of her eye, Belle studied Quinn. He was tapping on the steering wheel and whistling along to the song on the radio. Dating didn't mean a commitment. It was something grown-ups did all the time.

She was a grown-up and so was he. They could do this and be normal. Maybe then her sisters-in-law would leave her alone for a while. He was leaving soon, so maybe she could practice her social skills on him. It wouldn't be a real date.

She took a breath, turned to him, but closed her mouth when she looked over his shoulder.

A police car blocked their path.

Chapter Eight

Sheriff Cantu got out of his car and waved. Quinn had a bad feeling about this. He glanced at Belle. Her brow was creased.

"Do you have a clue what's going on?" he asked her.

"No. We weren't even on the street yet, so there was no way you performed a traffic violation. I hope everyone's all right." Worry edged her voice.

As the sheriff approached, Quinn rolled down the window. "How can we help you?"

Lowering his tall frame, Cantu made eye contact with Belle. "I was heading out to the ranch. I need you at the station. The Texas Rangers have a trailer full of freshly stolen cattle and want to see if you can identify them. They're tagged. Can you come now?"

Quinn was about to say yes but thought better of it. He glanced at Belle. "I can take you. If they're yours, we can get this over with today." The losers had stolen from her, and he wanted a pound of flesh, but it wasn't his place.

Tight-lipped, she nodded, and he followed the black-and-white SUV to the station in the middle of the tiny town. Inside, Sheriff Cantu introduced them to two Texas Rangers and the local game warden, Amanda Ortiz.

She shook their hands. "I found the truck behind the Seahorse Hotel. They've either gotten brave, lazy, or they're just not smart. I recognized Jacoby's brand and thought the heifers looked like yours. The Rangers—" she waved at the two men standing to the side "—Matt and Calvin, had just left, so I called them in and we confiscated the trailer. We found two guys and a woman. You're not going to be happy about a couple of them. At first, they claimed the owner asked them to move the cattle, but then they stopped talking."

"Do I know them?"

Calvin, the taller Ranger, handed her three pictures.

She gasped, and her legs went weak. Quinn moved to stand behind her, a hand on her waist, steadying her.

Grounded now, Belle's fingers shook only slightly as she handed the pictures back. "The woman and the blond guy work for me part-time. Whenever they need money, I find them work. They were living on the ranch, in one of the cabins. They were stealing from me?"

"Did they have permission to drive the cattle to Mexico?"

"No." Eyes closed, she lowered her head and rubbed her temples.

The warmth of Quinn's hand was on her shoulder now. He leaned close to her ear. "This is good. They were caught."

"They worked for me. I trusted them. Whenever they needed help, I would give it. I don't understand why they would do this to me."

Amanda sighed. "Easy money. But they won't have to worry about room and board for a while. Texas takes cattle theft very seriously. We have evidence that this isn't the first time, but they're working alone."

"Do you know how many you've lost?" Matt asked.

"We didn't realize they were being stolen at first. The numbers were small. At the beginning of the year, it was about five. Then we found the fence down and about forty were missing. Just yesterday, Damian said another fifty were gone. I reported all of them."

"These would probably be the fifty. Another fifty belong to Jacoby."

"Have you called him?"

"He's on his way in."

People she trusted did this. Her stomach hurt. "What happens now?"

Matt led them to a desk and went through the procedures. It felt as if they'd been there for hours when they were finally allowed to go.

"At least you'll get some of your cattle returned to you."

"Yeah, it could have been much worse. I'm just so angry at myself. How could I be so naive and not even suspect them?"

"You were trying to help. Don't beat yourself up over it."

"But it's my fault. I'm responsible for the ranch. I make the hiring decisions. I…" She closed her eyes. This was what happened when she got distracted, thinking she could have a relationship. Quinn wasn't the problem. She was.

Quinn gripped the steering wheel. He had planned on telling her about his mission on the way to the house, but now seemed like the worst time.

He maneuvered the Land Rover around the deep ruts on the ranch road. It really needed to be graded and re-surfaced with new caliche. But hey, he needed practice at avoiding potholes.

He sighed. There would always be a reason not to tell her. But his time was up. He couldn't go any longer without disclosing to Belle why he was in Port Del Mar. *Just tell her.*

He held in a groan. She had just found out that two people she had let stay on the ranch, people she had helped, had betrayed her.

There was a good chance she wouldn't want to talk to him ever again. Not even as a friend. And he didn't have any of those, either.

Reality sideswiped him. When had his life become devoid of all friendships? His knuckles turned white over the steering wheel.

After Kari's death, he hadn't had any energy. The girls had been confused and lost without their mom. He'd had a newborn baby. His mother-in-law had moved in to help, but her only child had just died, so she was deep in grief, too.

For months, he had let the Foundation flounder. It had been Kari's passion, her family's legacy, and she had shared it with him. Now it was up to him to see it through, to make sure it was solid enough to pass on to his kids, like he promised.

He was alone now in the responsibility to raise their children and grow the Foundation's reach. He was sur-prised at the flash of old anger. For months he'd been angry at God, at Kari and himself, but it was exhausting to live with that intensity of emotion, and it was hurting his children. The anger had no place in his life. It was behind him.

He couldn't afford to let himself get swallowed in old regret.

"Quinn." She twisted in her seat, and the warmth in her gaze taunted him. She was about to discover he had been keeping secrets. He was going to destroy her plans. The trust she had shown him would vanish. He was a jerk.

She cleared her throat, her hands making nervous gestures in her lap. "Quinn. This might sound… Well, I might be…" She took a deep breath.

He went on high alert as his mouth went dry. "What's wrong?"

"Oh. Nothing." She laughed. Not a real laugh, but the kind a person used when they wanted others to think everything was all right. "With everything that's happening, I want something good in my life, but I don't know."

"Belle. You should have tons of good in your life. Just spit it out. If there's a way I can help you, I will. You're a great person and you don't deserve what they did to you."

"Thank you. You know, in the past, I would have pulled into myself and shut everyone out. I want to try something else. Take action. Be bold." She gave a half-hearted fist pump into the air. Then she sighed. "I'm tired of living in fear and doubt."

"Okay." This was killing him. She looked so unsure of herself. He didn't like it.

"So, we're both single parents and we've become friends. I know you're leaving soon. I'm not looking for…" She dropped her eyes. "I'm making a total mess of this, which is obviously one of the many reasons I don't date."

"What does this have to do with dating?" Now he was totally confused.

With a dramatic sigh, she shifted back and lifted her chin. Suddenly she became very interested in the ceiling of his Land Rover.

The silence went on too long. "Belle? What's going on?"

"I had the lame idea that we could go on a date, but not a real date. Nothing big and fancy. I just haven't ever been on a date, and since we're friends, I thought you might be a safe place to start. Like a practice run." With a straining noise, she buried her face in her hands. "This is so humiliating. I shouldn't ever be allowed out in public with adults."

"You've never been on a date?" He didn't know there were new places in his heart that could break. She had no clue how adorable she was, and he didn't want to hurt her feelings again. After the orca comment, he needed to be extra careful. "You've been married and had two children. How does that happen?"

"Small town. Sad to say that it didn't take much to impress me. Jared and I hung out on the beach, cruised Main Street. We never went on a formal date, not even prom—I'd already had Cassie by then. But I thought we could… I could ask you. I don't want to do anything stupid and I'm not sure what…"

"Are you asking me if you can ask me on a date?"

Parking in front of his cabin, he killed the engine and sat there. She shifted; her fingers tangled.

He could keep his mouth shut a few more days. Not saying anything about the Commissioners Court or the fragile coastline she owned. They could go out as friends and pretend to have a normal life and enjoy the evening. Like two normal adults without heaping piles of baggage.

Belle had never been on a real date. There was no justice in that.

He hadn't been on a date since… Maybe it had been too long for him, too. He should make himself move on.

Muscles from his chest to his gut tightened from the inside out and every nerve in him screamed no. He didn't want to move on without Kari. He studied the woman sitting next to him. She was the first to have him seeing a life beyond his wife.

He wasn't prepared for the old feelings Belle stirred to life. And now she sat staring out the window, pretending she hadn't put herself out there for rejection.

It would be easier if he said yes. Easier in this moment, but not the long run. If he wanted his children to be adults with integrity, it started with him.

And if he had any chance of saving this relationship between them, of keeping her as a friend, he had to tell her the truth.

"My first instinct is to say yes. Yes, we should go on a date. We're friends and I would love to spend more time with you."

She crossed her arms over her middle. "I hear a huge 'but' somewhere in that sentence. It's okay. You don't have to let me down easy. I'm tough."

Tough because life had made her that way. He wanted to reach over and make everything right for her. To kiss her until the world didn't matter.

She deserved to be completely loved. But he wasn't that man.

"It's not about us. We need to talk about the reason I'm here in Port Del Mar."

A frown pulled at her forehead. "I thought it was for research on the Gulf Coast."

"It is. We're researching and investigating all the undeveloped land in this area of the coast and working to find ways to protect it from ever being developed."

Her head tilted in confusion at first. Then her eyes went wide, and she gasped, seeing the implications immediately. "You came to take the ranch?"

He couldn't look at her. "No, but the Diamondback has one of the last clean strips of coastal shore that hasn't been developed yet. When we found the ocelots, it was a huge bonus."

Eyes narrowed, she studied him a bit before speaking. "But if the land can't be developed, then I can't sell. No one will spend millions on land they can't build on."

"Right. These guys are losing their natural homes forever due to land being overdeveloped. We must protect our natural resources. Once they're gone, there's no going back."

Her hand went to her chest as if to slow a rapid heartbeat. "But it's my land. You can't do this."

"I'm sorry, Belle. But those orphaned cubs and the nesting sea turtles are all the proof I need to go forward with a petition to keep the land untouched. Your ranch is the perfect natural refuge. They're already here. I'll be presenting at the next county meeting with information about the endangered species this area serves. I'm looking for them to restrict use of the land."

The look of betrayal in those gray-green eyes hit him hard. This was not what he wanted.

Quinn banged his head against his seat. There had to be a way to make this work. He should have known that today's good mood couldn't last.

Of all the days to lose Belle's friendship, this would be it.

Soon they would have to join the kids and act like everything was fine.

This was one of those moments when he didn't want to be an adult.

Acid burned in her stomach.

This good-looking single dad had been too good to be true. It was all about him and what he wanted. Just like her ex-husband and her uncle. "You're trying to take my ranch from me."

"No. I just want to protect the shoreline."

"By stopping me from selling it. I can't save my ranch if I don't have that option. You even met the Realtor I'm listing with. You used me."

"Belle, don't. I didn't—"

They both jumped when someone banged on his window. "Daddy. Come here. The ocelots are awake. We want to feed them."

A tight smile on his face, he opened his door. "Okay, sweetheart. We'll be right there."

Hannah ran back to the cabin, yelling at everyone else. He turned to Belle, the forced smile gone. "Belle. I wasn't expecting you or the connection we—"

Hand up, she stopped any more words. "Don't. Your children need a home, and I'm not going to kick you off the property. But I would appreciate it if you'd stay away and not talk to me."

"What about the mornings?"

She groaned. He knew her weakness. "Are you using your children to—"

"No. The morning routine has become important to us…them. I'll stay out of your way, but don't punish them because you're mad at me."

"Daddy!" Hannah was back on the porch, this time surrounded by all the other kids.

Quinn gave Belle a long look, like this was somehow her fault.

She was the difficult one, right? The one who caused problems and didn't know her place. That had been said to her more than once.

She closed her eyes. She wasn't going to give him that power. She hadn't done anything wrong. Her family needed her to be strong and fight anything that threatened them. And fight she would.

"Daddy, hurry!"

He didn't break eye contact with her. She had to turn away and blink back the burn in her eyes. No crying. She shook her head, then got out of the Land Rover.

He sighed. "I'm coming."

Pausing at the side of his vehicle, she adjusted her ponytail. Why was she upset? She'd known how it would turn out. He was charming and pulled her in, then…wham!

Idiot must be stamped across her forehead.

She was not going to give up on the ranch. She'd call Xavier and Elijah. Damian didn't talk much, but he knew a lot of legal stuff. Maybe he'd help her.

Why did it hurt so much? She was smarter than this.

Tall, good-looking cowboys were bad life choices. Always had been, always would be. Instead of learning her lesson, she'd asked him on a date. He had to be laughing over that.

"Mom!" Cassie called out to her, and just like everyone else she followed Quinn into the cabin.

All the kids had gone very quiet as Quinn took them through the feeding. He gave each of the kids a job to help feed the cubs.

It wasn't fair; he made her feel like the bad guy. She agreed that the natural land and habitat were important and needed protection. But her family needed protection, too.

It had been her job alone to make sure her family had a place to call home. They had all left her at one point, but she made sure they all had a place where they could heal. She couldn't lose the ranch now. Elijah and Xavier were solid now, but Damian was still lost in his own world of pain.

What would he do if they had to walk away from the ranch? If they couldn't get the capital to make the ranch financially solid, where would she go?

The land was in her blood. It had given her reason to get up and stand on her own.

Jazz entwined her arm with Belle's, interrupting her thoughts. "He's amazing, isn't he? I mean, he loves his kids, takes care of his mother-in-law. She even likes him. And he loves animals. It's time you stepped out of your safe little box and asked him out."

She wanted to ignore her. Since Jazz had teamed up with Selena in the "Find Belle a Man" project, they had been pushing her to the edge. They meant well, and she knew it came from love, but they needed to put an end to it.

Jazz went on. "Your kids get along, and he lives right here on the ranch. Since we can hardly get you off Diamondback, he's perfect." She squeezed Belle's arm.

"I did ask."

Her sister-in-law's eyes widened, and she gasped. Elijah and a couple of the kids close to them turned. "Everything okay?" Elijah asked, bringing Quinn's attention to them.

Heat climbed Belle's neck, and she hung her head.

Jazz waved them off. "It's fine."

Then Jazz hugged her closer and whispered in her ear, "I'm so proud of you. Where are you going?"

"We're not. He's not interested."

"What?"

"Shhh." They were all looking at them again. "Please, not here. I'll tell you everything later." She wasn't ready to go into the whole ranch problem until she'd done some research.

Elijah came at them from one side, and Selena, with one of the triplets on her hip, joined them from the other. "What's going on?" she whispered.

"And why are we whispering?" Elijah kept an eye on Quinn and the kids. "You ladies are scaring me."

Could the ground just open and take her? For years she had wanted her family together and close by, but now she realized she didn't know what she'd been asking for.

"Everything's fine. Jazz is just being dramatic. We're here to see the ocelots. They're extremely rare, and few people get to see them."

Elijah didn't look like he was going to let it go. "Is

it the ranch? Did something happen with the rustlers they caught? Are you having problems?"

"No. Well, not anything you don't know about. We'll talk later."

He nodded, then studied his wife with concern. "Are you okay?"

Jazz was coming out of her first trimester, and Elijah tended to hover.

"I'm fine. I was asking—"

Belle glared at Jazz.

"Oh, yes. I was just... Well, everything's fine." Jazmine took Oliver from Selena. "I want to see these baby wildcats."

The babies that might have cost her the family ranch. But nothing was going to change right now, so Belle put her smile in place and went to her daughters.

Quinn's large hands were gently feeding one of the cubs. Her heart kicked against her chest. It was so scarred it should be numb by now. Not feeling anything would make life easier.

Quinn placed the little cat in the crate with its sibling.

Elijah came up behind her and took her elbow. He had his phone in his hand and gently pulled her away from the group. "Do I need to know what you and Jazz were talking about?"

She frowned. "No. Really, Elijah, don't overreact. It was no big deal."

"You sure it isn't connected to our mother?"

She pressed her lips together tight to stop herself screaming at him. "Why would it have anything to do with our mother?"

"I don't know." He held up his phone. "Xavier texted me. She's at the main house and is looking for you."

Chapter Nine

The world didn't make sense. Elijah's image blurred, and his words bounced off her brain as nonsense.

"Quinn." Her brother waved Quinn over. "Would you drive Belle to the main house and stay with her until the visitors are gone?" The word *visitors* came out as a sarcastic snarl.

"What's wrong? Is it the visitors?" Confusion was deep in each wrinkle on Quinn's forehead.

Processing what her brother had said, Belle turned from Quinn to glare at Elijah. "No! I'm not going alone. If I have to talk to Celia, you will be with me." Her throat was dry. "She's your mother, too."

Elijah had the nerve to pull her close and rest his forehead on hers. "I can't." His voice was low and rough, as raw as jagged glass. "I'm sorry, but my insides are a jumble of dark thoughts, and I need a chance to clear my head and be prepared before I stand in the same room as her."

What about my insides?

With a deep inhalation, he cleared his throat. "Find out what she wants. I'll take Jazz and Rosie home. Then

I'll come back you up. Please, Belle. I need the time to process. She didn't even ask for me." His deep, steady voice cracked. "She was just looking for you."

She sucked in air to stop from crying out. Why did that woman still have so much power to hurt them? "Maybe I need time to process, too."

"You're the strongest of all of us. You always have been. We wouldn't have survived without you. I promise, I'll be back tonight, and we can send her and her latest guy on their merry way. She has no business being here."

She bit her bottom lip, holding back tears. Why did she have to be the strong one all the time? Just for once, she wanted someone to take care of her. The one time she thought she'd found a Prince Charming, he turned into a bullfrog. A mean one.

"Okay. But I don't promise to play nice. What if she's here for her part of the ranch?" She was being attacked from all sides today.

With a deep breath, he took a step back. "Xavier and Damian own most of the land. You've kept it running for years now. We're not going to let her come in and take over. I'm sorry I can't go with you, but I know my limits and…" He blew out a hard breath. "I don't like the way I'm feeling right now."

Her hand still in his, she squeezed it before letting go. "I've got this for right now. But I'm counting on you and Xavier to join us soon. I'll text and let you know why she's here."

Quinn was watching them, a neutral expression on his face as he watched the family drama.

She turned from them and went to the door. "I don't need an escort."

"I drove you here." In a few long strides, he was beside her, then looked at Elijah. "What about the kids?"

"We've got them covered," Elijah replied. "Stay with her. Someone gave Jonah a croquet set for his birthday, so we'll set that up. I'll take the girls home with Jazz and Rosie. Belle?"

Elijah called to her as she opened the screen door to the back porch. She paused at the threshold but didn't look at him.

"I promise, I'll come back and stay with you until that woman leaves. We aren't letting her back into our lives."

Unable to talk past the knot in her throat, she nodded. She jogged down the steps and cut across the small yard. The air was heavy. Rain was hanging in the air, but not falling. She needed to run. The land around her blurred. Her mother showing up couldn't be good.

"Belle." Quinn was next to her. "Are you okay?"

She didn't want to talk, so she nodded and kept walking. A gentle touch stopped her. "My car's there." He pointed in the opposite direction. "Unless you want to walk to the house."

She didn't know what she wanted other than she did not want to see her mother. Once again, everyone had left her to deal with the mess. Except for Quinn. Why was he still here?

With a shake of her head, she moved to his Land Rover. Then she stopped. "You don't have to drive me home."

"I drove you here. You don't have your car."

She looked over her shoulder. "I can walk." Maybe it would clear her head.

"If you want to walk, that's fine. But I'm walking with you. Which is it?"

She sighed. "Why are you helping me?"

"We're friends. I don't understand why your mother being here is so upsetting, but this is not a happy family reunion. It's not something you should be left alone to do."

But she was alone.

Without another word, she climbed into his car. At first, they sat in silence, which suited her.

"There's something I don't understand. If this is so traumatic, why is he making you go alone? She's his mother, too."

"It's complicated."

"I'm starting to hate that word. You seem to be the one fighting everyone's battles. He's a grown man."

She didn't like the judgment she heard in his voice. "He's an alcoholic. It's been almost six years that he's been sober. It's best if he can avoid high levels of stress and conflict. He was with our mother longer and has more memories of her. That's not a good thing. He'll be fine. He needs a little time to get through the emotions before he sees her. That's what I'm doing. It's an exploratory mission. I'll go in first and gather the info so that we know what we're dealing with and what to do from here."

"It seems to me that a great deal of the work and worry for this family falls on your shoulders."

"Well, you're in town to shut down my family ranch, so I'm not sure you have any right to have an opinion of my family." Pressing her lips together, she forced herself to stop talking. Staring out the window, she crossed her arms. She knew that was rude, but she didn't have the energy to play nice. Not with someone who wanted to ruin any chance she had of making the ranch a success.

"You're right. I overstepped. Sorry. You seem to

shoulder an uneven amount of the burden of the ranch problems."

"They help when they can. My uncle made it hard for them to be on the ranch. Since his death, they've been much more involved. Without them, I wouldn't have been able to hang on this long." She couldn't look at him. "I don't know why you care. You'd be happy if I failed. Maybe my mother being here is perfect for your plans."

Trusting him had been too easy and now she was paying for it.

She gasped, then jerked toward him. Had he set her up? "Her being here doesn't have anything to do with you, does it?" Elijah had sent Quinn thinking he would support her. Had they played right into his hands?

"No." He pulled up to her house but didn't cut the engine. "You have no reason to trust me. I withheld the reason I was in town, but other than seeing her name on the public records, I don't know your mother. I've never communicated with her in any form. When we walk in there, I'm on your side."

She snorted.

His jaw flexed, and his knuckles strained as he tightened his grip on the steering wheel. A sure sign he was angry with her. Biting her lip, she regretted the noise she had made. Her uncle and Jared had both hated it when she snorted.

She'd never seen evidence that Quinn could be violent, but maybe some men were better at hiding it.

With an unexpected movement, he turned to her, hands in front of him. Out of old habits of survival, she flinched and pressed her back to the window. She looked down. Then hated herself. She said a quick prayer, then lifted her chin and made sure to look him in the eyes.

No man was ever going to make her cower again.

But the eyes she met were full of horror. He scowled at her and lowered his hands. "Belle?"

Exposed. He'd seen too much.

"I know you don't trust me after today, but I'd never hurt you."

She wanted to tell him it was too late—her stupid heart had let him in when she wasn't watching—but that would give him power over her. Besides, that wasn't what he'd meant.

With a sigh, he placed his hand on the leather covering the steering wheel. He studied the land stretched out in front of them. "I've never met your mother, but I can tell you that I don't like her. Whatever happens in there, I'm on your side."

Great. Now she wanted to cry. She could not walk into the house in this weakened state. "Thank you."

He turned off the engine and went to open his door.

"Can we sit here for a bit? I need a little time to collect my thoughts."

"Sure." His door closed, and he studied her house. "Belle, you're a great mother. This home is full of love and welcomes people because of you. Just because she gave birth to you does not make her your mother. A mother should be a blessing, not someone who terrorizes her children to the point they don't want to meet her." He turned his attention to her. "When was the last time you saw her?"

"She left me here when I was six. She came back a couple of times. Maybe I was twelve. I don't remember."

"Did she call? Write?"

"No. She kept Elijah with her longer. The man she said was his father was in and out of her life, so she used Elijah until a blood test proved otherwise. He was eight or nine. Then he was useless to her. She's selfish—and you're right. She doesn't deserve the title 'mother.'"

He whistled and shook his head. "I don't even understand how a parent can—"

"It's in the past. What I need to deal with right now is the present. I need to find out why she's here." She looked at him. "You don't have to go with me."

"I'm not letting you go in there alone."

"Thank you." That meant more to her than it should.

Deep breath in, then she nodded. "I'm ready." She stepped out of the Land Rover and moved to the ranch house. Her home now. She wasn't the scared little girl left behind.

The ground sucked at her feet with each step. She reminded herself that she was strong and independent. No matter what her mother brought to her house, she would survive.

God had her. Everyone else might abandon her, but God held her close. He loved her. If she lost the ranch, that just meant that something else, something better, was waiting for her.

She couldn't imagine life without the land, but God was in control. Quinn moved behind her and softly laid a hand on her back. She stiffened.

Her heart should have known there was no happy-ever-after for her.

For a brief second, she had dreamed of more with Quinn. But like her other dreams, it was a false hope.

Chapter Ten

Quinn stayed close to Belle as they went into the house. Her mother sat at the kitchen table like it was hers. She was a handsome woman. He wasn't sure what he'd expected, but this elegant woman in her early fifties wasn't it.

Her dark hair was cut in a sleek bob that framed her face, its streaks of silver looking intentional. Her shirt was a bright yellow, and the tight jeans she wore had rips at the knees. She was smaller than Belle, almost a foot shorter and fragile-looking, with none of Belle's strong, bold stance.

She didn't look like someone who'd abandoned her children. He wasn't sure what a horrible mother should look like, but Celia De La Rosa wasn't it.

A younger-looking man was sitting next to her, scrolling through his phone.

Celia stood and rushed Belle, arms extended. "Izabella! Randy, this is my little ding-dong." She laughed. "Everyone called her Belle, so I thought 'ding-dong' was so cute." She wrinkled her nose as if something smelled bad.

Belle stiffened. She didn't look happy about the insulting nickname. She still hadn't said a word. Her back bumped his chest when she stepped away from the woman's hug. His hands went to her shoulders.

Celia dropped her arms and pretended she hadn't been snubbed by her daughter. "You've made several changes. I like it. It's brighter."

"What are you doing here?" The low guttural sound didn't sound like the Belle he knew.

"Oh, baby girl. I heard Frank died. I thought you needed me." Her gaze roamed around the room.

He wanted to ask her why she'd waited so many years, because he was sure her daughter had probably needed her for years. The minute her uncle started treating her like an unwanted stray, perhaps. Then again when her husband walked out on her and his children.

Now, not so much.

"There is nothing I need from you." Stronger now, Belle took a step away from Quinn.

"Oh, sweetheart." Her mother moved to the table. "Come on in and sit with us. There's so much to catch up on. This is Randy Anderson. My husband."

The man looked up and nodded at them. He finally set his phone aside. "It's a pleasure to meet Celia's family."

"You're married?"

"Yes. A year in May," he said.

"And you?" Celia gave Quinn a curious glance. He didn't like her calculating smile.

Belle walked to the table but didn't sit. Instead, she gripped the back of one of the red farm chairs. "Why are you at the ranch?"

"Randy thought it was a good time for me to check

on my property. You know Frank and I didn't get along. He disapproved of me. He made my life so difficult that I couldn't come home."

Quinn had planned to stay silent, but there was too much that needed to be said. "But it was okay for your children to be left here?" Heat started at his core. How could this woman sit there like she'd done nothing wrong? Acting as if she were the victim?

Belle reached for his hand.

"Sorry." He looked directly at her, making it clear that he was apologizing to her, not the woman at the table. "I overstepped. This is your conversation."

"Yes, you did," the man, Randy, said. "This is between mother and daughter. Who are you?"

"Dr. Sinclair." He never tossed his title around to impress people, but this pair brought out a darker side of him. He was going to have a serious talk with Elijah about throwing his sister to hungry sharks.

"You're married to a doctor? That's won—"

"No. He's on the ranch doing research." Belle lifted her chin. "What do you want?"

With a pout that was out of place on a grown woman, Celia leaned back in her chair. "I wanted to visit a bit. Where's Xavier and Damian? Are they interested in selling the ranch?"

Belle's whole body stiffened. "The ranch is our family home and, thanks to you leaving us here, it's the only home we know. You don't have any business here."

"That's not true. Come on and sit with me and we can talk." Celia patted the chair next to her. "If it's money you're worried about, I'm more than willing to give you some after the sale."

"No." Each breath sounded more labored. Celia stood

and took Belle's fisted hand, trying to pull her away from Quinn.

His fingers tightened around hers. The desire to wrap his arms around her was ridiculous. He dropped his hand.

Belle sat across from Randy as Celia slid in next to her. Wanting to stay close, Quinn took the chair on the other side of Belle. He wasn't sure why he was so worried about her; she'd made it clear to her mother that he was just here for research.

With the earlier information, he had been removed from the friend list, just one step below this woman who had no right to use the title of mother.

Randy leaned forward, crossing his arms. "You do realize it's worth millions? Seven million, to be exact. The strip along the coast hasn't been touched. It's got so much potential for development."

Belle glanced at Randy. A smoldering heat Quinn had never seen should have burned the man to a crisp.

"Oh, don't look at him that way." Celia swatted at Belle's arm. "He's just looking out for us. This land has always been more of a burden. It's holding you back. It tried to do the same to me, but I wouldn't let it. Think of what we could do with that kind of money. Frank wouldn't let me sell, but he's gone now. Don't let him hold you back, too."

Stiffly, Belle stayed on the edge of the seat. "I realize it doesn't mean anything to you. *We* don't mean anything to you, but this is everything for me. It's my home. My girls' home. We won't let you sell."

"Girls? You have daughters? Oh, sweetheart." Celia had tears in her eyes as she laid her hand over Randy's. "Did you hear that? I'm a grandmother. Randy has three grandsons, and I love spending time with them, but you have girls. How fun."

"No. You're not a grandmother, because you're not my mother. You left us with Frank and Mari. Mari raised us. She was the only mom I've ever known." Belle had her hand on the edge of the table, ready to push away. Quinn eased his hand under hers so that their fingers were intertwined.

He didn't care what these strangers thought. Belle needed a hand to hold, and he was the only one here standing by her side.

Those steady hands of hers shook. But one glance at her face and all anyone would see was a woman in control of her world. Strong and determined, she hid the fear that was running through her veins. She was a warrior protecting her family. He squeezed her hand.

"Oh, don't be like that. I did the best I could. I'm here now."

"You want me to believe that dropping us off with Frank was the best you could do? That was one step above dumping us on the side of the road and driving off."

"That's not true. Frank could be… Well, Frank could be difficult, but he loved this ranch. I knew that, if nothing else, he'd give you a home. You'd have a place to stay and a school to attend. This was a good place for you to grow up."

The gray overtook the green in Belle's eyes. Her glare was cold, hard steel. "Most of the time, once Mari died, he wouldn't even let us in the house. There was a shed between here and the barn, with a dirt floor." Her voice cracked, and her fingers tightened around

Quinn's. "I can't count all the times he locked us in there with nothing to eat."

A sound of distress came from Celia. A hand covered in silver jewelry went to her red lips.

Belle's chin went higher. "I waited for you. I cried and prayed to God for you to get us. I didn't understand why you had left us with him."

Her mother's eyes went wide. "No. What did you do that made him do that? Was it Elijah? He was always causing problems."

There was no way this woman had just tried to justify a man locking children in a shed. Quinn glanced at Belle. Her face was pale, and she blinked rapidly.

He moved closer to her so she knew she wasn't alone. There was no way he would remain silent. "Would you seriously blame a child for a horrific act done by an adult? There is no excuse for doing that to innocent children. None. Ever."

Belle placed a warm hand on his chest. "It's okay."

"No, it's not. That is never okay."

"You're right. I didn't mean what he did was okay. I'm okay. Right here and now. I'm okay. Thank you."

He wasn't sure she was as okay as she claimed. Earlier today, he had threatened her home. His plan would destroy any chance of her goal to build a safe place for her family.

Guilt and shame left a nasty taste in his mouth.

Belle studied Quinn. She should hate him, but now she wanted to get lost in his arms and hide. What if she reached up and kissed him?

She was off balance, and it was all Celia's fault. Otherwise, she wouldn't be seeing the strength in Quinn. He was in town for one reason, and getting to know her was just one part of it.

But now he was suddenly her only support. Quinn was the only one who was standing next to her as she faced the woman who'd given birth to her and then abandoned her. The woman she never wanted to see again was in her house, threatening everything she held dear, but pretending she was doing it for her family.

Glancing down, she studied the details of the sun-kissed skin of the man who should be her enemy but was standing with her.

Earlier, he had wanted to block the future for her children, to interfere with her ranch and life for different reasons. Now he was fighting for her.

Could she trust him, or was it all part of the act to get what he wanted? He might be more dangerous to her heart than her mother.

She heard her name and looked across the room at Celia. Her lips were moving. "That should have never happened. I never would have left you if I had known. He was always grumpy and disagreeable. But he wasn't violent like our father."

She approached Belle with her hands out. "I thought about you every day. The image of you and Elijah on the ranch playing, being free and going to school with friends at Port Del Mar made me happy. I wanted you to have roots in a place that you could call home. Is that so bad?"

Stepping away from Quinn, she made sure to stand on her own as she addressed her mother. "One call. One short trip home and you would have seen the truth. But you didn't want the truth, did you? It was easier to pretend we were having a great time, so you could… I don't even know what you were doing."

"I was born to be a singer. I won state competitions. I had dreams that my father didn't support. Frank laughed at me. Told me that I'd be begging for his help, but he wasn't gonna give it. But when he married Mari, I had an ally for the first time. You can't tell me Mari didn't love you. She loved you and Eli like you were her very own. She wanted you and loved you better than I could."

Her gut tightened. There had been a mother in her life, a woman she never told how much she loved her. "Yes. She was the only mother we ever had, and then she died." Tears burned her eyes. No, she would not cry in front of this woman. Celia didn't deserve any part of her, even the sad, messed-up parts. Mari deserved all her grief. Not this woman.

With a sudden realization, she looked at the old drugstore milkshake machine that had been Mari's. She had been a good mother to her. The kind of mother she wanted to be for her girls. But Belle hadn't told her she loved her, not even a thank-you.

The worst of Frank's actions had all happened after Mari died. That was when the nonstop drinking started. But it didn't matter. He was the adult and had needed to figure out a way to take care of them.

She looked at the woman who had abandoned them. "It doesn't change the fact that you dumped us and ran and never looked back. Now your husband is interested in the ranch and you care about my future? I don't buy it and I'm gonna fight any way I can to stop you from getting any part of this ranch. You'll hand it over to him and then he'll leave you like every other man in your life, except he'll take our ranch."

The man in question crossed his arms. "I'm looking

after your mother's best interests. She owns half of this ranch. That's just the facts."

"She has nothing to do with this ranch. She walked away years ago. And if she told you half the ranch is hers, she lied. Big surprise there."

"Half should be mine. Just because I was a girl Dad left most of it to Frank. It wasn't fair. I want my half."

"Then you should have stayed and fought for it. I kept it running when Uncle Frank fell apart. I'm the one who held everything together when the boys left. My blood, sweat and tears are in the land. You will not take it from me. I've sacrificed too much to lose it now."

Huge, fat tears fell from her mother's eyes, making the color brighter. "Baby, that's exactly why I'm here to help you. The men in this family don't appreciate their women. To them, we don't count. This piece of land is not worth giving up your life. Don't you have dreams? Did you even get to leave for college? What kind of future are you giving your girls?"

Quinn walked over to Belle and gently took her shaking hand in his. He stood next to her but stared at the crying woman across from them. "This is Belle's home. You said you left her here so that she would have a place to belong. Now you're telling her it's not worth it. Make up your mind."

Belle squeezed his hand. "We're done. I've said everything I wanted to say." She hadn't even realized until now how much she had wanted to scream at her for leaving them. So much resentment she had buried and denied. She let it go. Her shoulders relaxed; the weight lifted.

Her life was right where she wanted it and she wasn't going to allow the past to take anything from her future.

"Give me your number and I'll call you so we can

meet with everyone. From now on, if you want to talk to me, you do it with Elijah, Xavier and Damian, as well. Where are you staying?"

With a frown, Celia tilted her head. "We're staying here."

"No. You can stay in Port Del Mar, or across the bridge." She slid a pad of sticky notes and a pen across the table. "Write down your number and one of the boys will call."

"I'm not ready to leave."

Belle went to the door and opened it.

Randy took her mother's hand and led her to the porch.

Celia stopped and looked at her. "I could go with you to meet the gir—"

"No." She stared her down. "You need to leave. I don't want you on the ranch unless you're invited."

Quinn joined her on the edge of the porch. They stood in silence, watching until the car was out of sight. She hated that she drew comfort knowing he was near.

She looked at her phone to check the time. She should call Elijah, but she was too tired. If she talked to him now, she would do something stupid, like sob.

What she really wanted to do was curl up under the quilt Mari had made and pretend she was in her arms while she cried like a baby. She missed Mari so much. She was her mom.

But she wasn't here and there was no time for that weakness. Too many problems to fix.

A gentle touch on the center of her back caused her to jump.

"Quinn." Her hand went to her chest.

"Sorry. I didn't mean to scare you. Is there anything I can do to help?"

"No." Her breath caught and her chest tightened. She was losing everything.

"I never wanted you to lose the ranch. That wouldn't solve anyone's problems." He looked away. "I'm not sure I've ever met someone so completely out for herself at the expense of everyone and everything else."

"That's human nature. We all have agendas and are working to get what we each want. I understand." She didn't, but it was what she had learned to expect.

"Really? We'll have to agree to disagree because the last thing you need right now is another argument. Okay. Change of subject. Do you want alone time, or do you need your family?"

"Family always comes first." The words were harsh and angry, but she was too tired to play nice.

"That's true, but to take care of your family, you need to be at full strength. That means taking care of yourself. What do you need?" He stood in front of her, blocking the view of her ranch. His eyes challenged her to speak the truth and not hide. It was so much easier for her if he didn't see the real Belle.

She was tired of being the one who had to solve all the problems. For once, she wanted someone to take over, someone to tell her that it would all be fine.

His hand came up but then dropped. The longing to lean into him and let those strong arms hold her startled her and ran so deep that it scared her.

There was no time to curl up in a ball and hide. The problems had to be dealt with head-on. Unfortunately, Quinn Sinclair was one of those problems.

His fingers brushed a strand of hair back from her face, the tips barely grazing her skin, but the warmth shot to her toes.

"My gut tells me—" his voice was soft and sooth-ing against her battered heart "—that you need a little bit of alone time to regroup. I'll keep the kids and tell Elijah that you'll call him when you're ready."

She sighed with relief. That was what she needed—a chance to recharge without anyone looking at her, ex-pecting her to have all the answers.

Right now, she didn't have any. She was empty. "An hour would be good. Thank you."

His lips brushed her cheek. On instinct, she turned and found his lips. She craved to be connected in a way that she had denied herself for so long. He stiffened for a moment, and the muscles in his upper arms tightened as if he was going to pull back. She had made a mistake.

Then he relaxed. His lips moved over hers in full possession. His fingertips touched each side of her jaw, holding her in place with a gentle control. All the anxi-ety and confusion slipped away from her as she moved closer into his warmth. Never in her life had someone cherished her like Quinn was in this one kiss.

Her defenses were low. Taking comfort from his strength for one moment wasn't going to undermine her. It was a moment for herself. Then she would go back to standing alone.

His hand moved to her nape. A soft sound vibrated in his throat as he moved to kiss her along the jaw.

Pulling him closer, she absorbed his strength and gentleness. What was she doing? Squeezing her eyes shut, she balled her hands over his chest.

As much as she wanted to lose herself in him, she couldn't. One deep breath, and she took three steps back. "You have a job to do, and I have my family ranch to save. This didn't mean anything."

"Belle—"

Crossing her arms, she turned from him. "It was a moment of weakness. I'm sorry if you took it as something more."

"There is nothing weak about you. In over ten years I've only wanted to kiss one woman and she was my wife. Don't belittle my feelings by saying it didn't mean anything." His hand went to her shoulder. "I get it. You see me as one of your enemies right now, but don't tell me this is nothing. We'll put it on hold, but we will revisit this thing between us."

His warmth tugged at her as he stepped closer. His hands went to her upper arms. "Belle, we—"

"No. Even if we find a way to get around our opposite goals, you're leaving in the next few months. Neither one of us can afford a casual fling. We have children, and they'll get attached." She stepped from him, her arms wrapped tightly around her middle. "I have cattle thieves, a long-lost mother and saving the ranch to deal with." She waved her hands. "No time for this."

He gave her a nod and went down the steps, then paused. "I'll leave, but I'm not leaving you. It's going to be okay."

"You don't know that. Sometimes life doesn't work the way it is supposed to. That's a lesson you know better than anyone."

His mouth was set in a grim line. "Yeah." His expression closed off.

She was tired and couldn't read his expression. "I'm sorry."

"Get some rest." He left.

Not sure why, she stood on the top step until his Land Rover was out of sight. Feelings couldn't be trusted. They steered her wrong every time.

No one was going to fight for her and her girls like she could. Elijah and Xavier had her back when they could, but they had their own issues to deal with.

Going to her room, she pulled her Bible from the side table. It had been too long since she spent any real time in prayer.

Between Quinn and her mother, everything she had worked so hard to build was about to fall apart.

God was the only way through this mess. She had lost her faith after Mari died, but God was always faithful. She went to her knees and opened her heart, giving everything over to Him.

Chapter Eleven

Quinn made a point to return each stare with a pleasant smile. There were more people at the County Commissioners Court than usual, but that was normal whenever landowners' rights versus environmental issues were on the agenda. He had a feeling he would be seen as the bad guy.

He focused on the papers in front of him. The map highlighting sensitive areas in the county screamed silently at him. The Diamondback Ranch was the key to his plans. It was easy to say that land needed to be protected, but when that protection hurt families, it wasn't as clear-cut. There had to be a way to save both.

Maybe he was missing something that could help all of them.

Never once in all his time defending the coastline and natural resources had he been this nervous. It was too personal. He looked across the room and studied her.

Belle's worn denim was replaced with the light green floral dress he'd seen only on Sundays. The usual tight braid was gone. Her thick dark hair was clipped on top and fell down her back in long waves. The soft, feminine appearance was an illusion. He knew how strong and stubborn she was at her core. How strong she thought she had to be, anyway.

Xavier had his arm around her as they talked in low voices. Quinn wanted to be the one to encourage her and support her. But that was impossible right now.

She saw him as the enemy.

The last few days, she had made sure to avoid him. Which left him feeling strange. Belle had worked her way into his heart and mind. He was bouncing between guilt and weird happiness. There was no way this could end well for them all.

This morning, as the kids had prepared to head over to the ranch to help with the animals, Gina had caught him whistling.

He hadn't whistled since his son was born. Regret had shut him down again when he'd realized what his mother-in-law's smile meant.

He used to whistle all the time. It had annoyed Kari, but he would laugh and tell her she brought too much joy into his life not to whistle.

It had been five years, but he was whistling again. Belle and he might not have a future, but she had taught him an important lesson. He could honor the promise he made to his wife and love her while living his life in full.

He could love again. Maybe in the next few years, the timing would be right. The kids would be older, and he could be in a real relationship again. He missed his wife, but he also missed the companionship.

Elijah slipped into the chair next to him. "You don't have to bring this to a public hearing tonight. With our mother just showing up, Belle doesn't need more shadows to fight. She needs a friend."

With a glare, Quinn let him know he wasn't having happy thoughts about the De La Rosa men and the way they had abandoned Belle. "And she could have used a brother when meeting with that woman. Did you finally meet with your mother?"

The other man looked down. "Yes. Not that it did any good." He brought his gaze up. "But we're talking about what you're doing to Belle. This is so unfair to her. She counted you as a friend and she doesn't do that easily."

More reason to carry guilt around. "I know. Which is one reason *I* stayed with her when she faced your mother. She shouldn't have had to do that alone. At least you're here for her tonight." He had more opinions on the subject, but he'd already said too much. It wasn't his place to get involved in family drama.

Belle's brother turned away from him. "That was my bad. It won't happen again." He gestured to the front of the room where the court would sit, including Xavier's wife, Selena, who was a commissioner.

"But I don't get how you could act like her friend and then do this. Trust doesn't come easy to her. She let you into her family."

He didn't want to take it to a higher court, but with a De La Rosa in the decision-making process, he might not get the support from the local entity like he hoped. Did Selena regret introducing him to Belle? Pulling himself back, he made direct eye contact with Elijah. "I don't do this lightly."

"You could still excuse yourself and not speak today," Elijah suggested.

"I can't do that. This project has been in motion for

over a year. Now your mother's the biggest threat to the ranch. She wants to get the most money any way she can, and if we get the land protected, she'll be cut off. If they agree to investigate my petition, the land sale will be put on hold. That'll buy Belle time. Your mother can't even take a loan against the land."

Elijah sat back, jaw flexing. "We hadn't considered her taking that action."

Quinn cut a glance at Belle. She quickly jerked her head in the opposite direction. She had been staring at him. "Yeah, I don't see her having a problem getting the loan, then letting the bank take ownership of the ranch when she stops making payments."

Elijah's fist tightened around the brim of his hat resting against his leg. "She'd do that, wouldn't she?"

"That's exactly what she would do. It would be the fastest way for her to get money." Quinn rubbed his forehead and sighed. "I don't want to hurt Belle. If I could come up with another plan to protect the habitat while helping Belle, I'd do it."

Surprised, Elijah glanced across the room at Belle. "Have you told her?"

"No. I don't give empty promises, and right now, I don't have enough to form a basic plan."

"Talk to her. She's smart and could see things you don't."

Tara, one of the Foundation's scientists, cleared her throat.

"Elijah, this is Tara. She and a small team with the Foundation came in from Houston yesterday."

Tara gave him a polite smile, then turned to Quinn. "I have a couple of adjustments I want to show you."

Taking his leave, Elijah joined his family on the other side of the room.

Quinn was relieved to see Belle surrounded by her family today. He knew she had been dreading this town meeting. Turning his attention to Tara, he tried to listen as she once again went through the data she had organized and prepared for him to present. Calling her meticulous would be an understatement. It would be easier to let her do this, but that would be cowardly of him.

He had made the connections in town, collected local information and designed the program and suggestions. The people knew his face. He was the one who needed to stand in front of them and tell them why he was here.

Quinn forced himself out of his own head and regarded the roomful of people, most of whom he knew. Even Belle's grumpy neighbor, Jacoby, was here.

Port Del Mar was the first place his family had wanted to make home, a place where they belonged.

People he wanted to claim as friends stared at him. The familiar faces ranged from curious and suspicious to downright hostile. They were all waiting for him to speak. Wanting to know what he was doing in their town.

This was the first place his kids had asked to stay. They loved the ranch and had friends. The girls got upset at the thought of leaving the horse club they had become a part of with Belle and her girls. That was the problem with getting involved and making connections; you didn't want to leave.

But the promise he had made to Kari couldn't be broken. The Foundation could make an impact, and it was part of his children's legacy, too.

Tara nudged him and raised an eyebrow. He had been

so lost in his thoughts that he'd forgotten where he was. Time to get his job done.

Hard stares waited for him to speak. If he couldn't get local support in other places, he moved to higher courts. That wouldn't work here. He didn't want to make enemies of the people who had called him friend. He glanced over his shoulder. Belle would never forgive him.

Another plan started coming together in his mind. He scribbled a few notes quickly, then handed the piece of paper to Tara. She lifted a brow. With a grin, he nodded and mouthed for her to start the research.

With a deep breath, he approached the podium and gave his arguments for the protection of the fragile coastline. They were based on solid facts, but this plan would hurt Belle. He might be moving on to a new location, but he couldn't walk away leaving Belle's dreams broken.

Belle listened to every word Quinn spoke. Each syllable was so smooth and prepared. He answered every question with facts and a clear certainty that leaving the land undeveloped was the only option for the future of the wildlife that depended on their strip of coastland.

His voice showed his Texas roots but was flavored with the world travel he had done. She could listen to him all day. Everything he said sounded right and good.

If it hadn't been her land in question, she would have supported him, but it was her livelihood, and she couldn't let him take that from her and her family.

He was a tough act to follow. She wanted to hide, but instead, she gripped the edge of the podium and spoke from her heart.

The first few questions were easy. Damian had prepared her with pertinent Texas legislation, which leaned in favor of the private landowner, but it made her feel like the bad guy when she thought of the baby ocelots and sea turtles.

The last few questions were not so easy. One of the newer officials asked about the developers who were looking at the land and their plans for it.

Her throat was dry as she told them she wasn't sure. That would be their decision to make, but she had to admit the land wasn't likely to be left alone.

The hands on the clock had to have stopped a couple of times. How long was she going to stand here and answer questions? Sweat rolled down her spine.

She hated this. All she wanted was to be out on the ranch working with her hands, not standing in flimsy shoes at a stuffy community meeting.

Selena surprised her the most. She had to recuse herself on the vote, since it was her family's property, but could give input.

There were a few softer questions about how she used the land for ranching now, and then, after what seemed like five hours, she stepped from the podium and found a quiet spot in the rear.

A few people spoke after her, including her neighbor, Jacoby. Growing up as a De La Rosa, it was more common to have the town angry at them for something her uncle did. Her heart beat harder and her throat burned as they took turns supporting her. That was unexpected. She blinked back the tears that threatened to fall.

The commissioners started on their agenda. They agreed that they needed more information and discussion before they voted on Quinn's petition for the coastal land to be restricted from any development. It was on hold for now. They would place it on the agenda for next month. Her heart raced. She had another month of not being able to move forward with her plans.

She closed her eyes. Another month of not knowing. Which was still better than an outright yes to Quinn.

Most of the people left, and a few other agenda items were discussed and voted on. Then the meeting was called to an end.

She slipped out the side door before anyone could talk to her. There was nothing they could say that would make this better, and she couldn't deal with people right now.

Standing at her truck, she dug in her purse for her keys. Where were they? She hated it when she didn't make sure they were in the side pocket. She looked through the window to make sure she hadn't left them in the truck. Her brain had been going over all the points she had wanted to make, so there was no telling what she had done with them.

No. They weren't in the ignition. She emptied her purse on the hood. Footsteps came up behind her. She spun around, not sure who she was expecting, and found Selena and Xavier.

She didn't want to talk to anyone, especially her cousin-in-law. Her emotions were too close to the surface.

Xavier put an arm around her. "Did you lose your keys? We can give you a ride home. You have an extra set there, don't you?"

"They're here somewhere." Tears burned the backs of her eyelids. She hated being incompetent and needing help. "I have to figure things out on my own, anyway. That meeting didn't go well."

She glanced at Selena, hating the betrayal that burned. The woman she counted as a sister. The guilt in Selena's eyes made it worse.

Selena joined her and carefully organized the notebooks, receipts, scissors, a variety of lip balms and all the other odds and ends that had been stored away in the big leather bag.

"You understand why I didn't speak, right? As a member of the court and a family member, I won't be able to vote because of a conflict of interest."

"Sure." She stuffed the items back into the bag. The keys weren't there.

"Hey." Selena put a hand on her arm to stop her movement. "It's going to be okay. No matter what happens, you and the girls are going to be okay. Xavier and I won't let anything happen to y'all."

"You can't say that. The ranch's future is up in the air and you can't guarantee that we will win this battle."

"You're not the ranch. There is so much more to you. You need to trust that God has this."

"The ranch is the only thing I know." Her eyes stung and her lungs hurt. "God's plans haven't worked out so well for me so far." She wanted to yell at Selena that just because she got her happy ending didn't mean everyone did.

That smacked of self-pity. She'd never given in to it before and she wasn't going to now.

Selena put an arm around her shoulders and squeezed. "Well, I do have a plan. You know what we need to do? Easter is in two weeks and we haven't done anything to prepare. Come on. I just happen to have a car loaded with supplies and a family ready to make a piñata and *cascarones.* We need to get ready for Easter, and the kids love making—"

"Belle." They all turned at the sound of Quinn's voice. In long strides, he cut across the now empty parking lot. "Are these yours?" He held up the key chain with the fluffy purple heart Cassie had made at summer camp.

A couple of the people who had sat with him were close behind. He had a whole team now to take her down. Holding her last meal in its place was hard, but she had faced worse and persevered. She'd survive Quinn Sinclair, too.

She took the keys with a nod. "Thanks."

His fingers brushed hers, reminding her of the warmth he had offered her not long ago. When she had had that moment of hope that she could trust again. Had he done that on purpose?

Pulling back, she glanced at the small crowd now standing around her truck. "I'll be going now." Keys in hand, she clicked the fob to unlock the doors.

"Hold on, Belle." Quinn stepped closer to her and braced his hand on her car door.

Was he serious? She glared at him.

He twisted to look behind him to a woman she didn't recognize. "Tara, have you heard anything?"

He faced her, then shifted his gaze to Xavier and Selena before making eye contact with her again. "This is Tara Garza. She works with the Foundation. Behind her is Nate Moore. They've been looking into our project here at Port Del Mar."

Tara's phone went off and she stepped away. Nate greeted everyone, then took his leave. Quinn's chest expanded as he sucked in a long, slow breath. His attention was riveted to the horizon over the hood of her old work truck. Finally, he swung back to her. "Belle, we need to talk."

"No." Using her truck for support, she hid behind closed eyes. There was no way she could talk to him as if they were friends.

"Can we go get something to drink at the Painted Dolphin?" he asked. "I shared some information with Elijah and realized I haven't done a good job of talking to you. I don't want to give you any false hope, but maybe we can work together and find an alternate plan that works for both of us."

She narrowed her eyes. "What are you talking about?"

"What I gave them tonight might not get approved. There are members who would rather run me out of town than listen to me. Your mother could undercut you, too. We'd both lose." He ran his fingers through his already rumpled hair. "What if we worked together? How could we get you what you need while saving the coastline? As a side benefit, we could cut your mother off from having access to the land."

Xavier crossed his arms. "Is this for real? You're not just messing with her?"

Quinn kept his gaze on Belle. "I promise I'm doing my best to help us both. Let's all go to the restaurant and talk."

Before she could respond, Tara joined them. "Andy said he has some basic information about land trust and is emailing it to you. He's going to dig a little further, and you should have all the information by the end of the week. Is there anything else you need from me?"

"No. Thank you for looking into it."

With a nod, Tara slipped her phone into her bag. "I'll

see you in the morning." She turned to Belle and her family. "It was a pleasure meeting you. I'm sure this will work out. Quinn's the best at finding solutions for difficult situations."

The thumping of Belle's heart rushed to her ears. He was looking for a solution to their situation? Hope was a very dangerous thing.

She waited, watching his every move as he spoke with Tara and then pulled out his phone.

Quinn was scrolling over the screen. Her jaw hurt from biting down. Was he torturing her on purpose?

"Quinn?" She glanced at Xavier. "What's going on?"

Xavier shrugged. Selena shook her head. She didn't know, either.

After what seemed like hours, Quinn looked up at her. The tentative smile wasn't very reassuring. "I have a proposal for you. Where's Elijah? It would be better if we could all go over this together."

Xavier moved closer to her and his shoulder touched hers. "He's at the Painted Dolphin." He lowered his head and gave her a look that asked for her opinion.

Patting his arm, she nodded. "That works for me." At this point, she didn't want to meet with Quinn alone. Her emotions were unstable, and the last thing she wanted was to break down in front of him. Really, she wanted to run. The betrayal was too fresh.

Was there something wrong with her that she developed feelings only for men who would hurt her?

This wasn't about her heart. They were talking solutions. Not that they would be ones that worked for her. But they were talking. Avoiding hard facts had never helped in the past.

Like every other obstacle in her life, it only got worse until she decided to charge at it straight on.

She'd waited too long for Jared to become a better man. She'd waited too long to make changes on the ranch.

She didn't hesitate now. Once she knew what she wanted, she made it happen. She wanted her ranch, and she didn't want the complication of having a man in her life.

"I'll meet you there." She swung the key chain around her finger, then climbed into her truck. She drove away from the three of them without a backward glance. She needed to be alone.

At the end of the parking lot, she gave in and glanced in the rearview mirror.

Quinn was talking with his hands. Xavier didn't look happy, but Selena had a hand on his chest. She looked to be pleading with him.

Putting her gaze on the road, she turned up the radio as her favorite song, "Voice of Truth," came across the airwaves. The tears she loathed fell, one lone trail, but then it started a flood, and there was no stopping them.

She patted her truck's dashboard. "We've gotten through much worse than this, right? We'll keep moving forward."

Just once, it would be nice not to have to fight for what she wanted. Would it be too much to ask for one battle to go her way, without all the stress?

"God, is there something You need from me? I lay it all at Your feet. I want to fight and keep the ranch, but if You have other plans, then show me those. I just want peace in what You give me. God, let me keep my heart and eyes open to You."

Chapter Twelve

Quinn stepped into the beachside restaurant that Elijah and Xavier owned. Several brightly colored sculptures of leaping dolphins hung from the ceiling. Large glass panels on one wall were rolled up like garage doors. The deck sat over the water. Boats were coming and going along the pier.

Searching the area, he found the De La Rosa family seated at a long table on the far corner of the deck. Selena was missing.

Elijah had joined them. Quinn was not able to get a read on him.

A waitress had brought a large pitcher of lemonade and bowls of chips and salsa. As the group spotted him, Xavier stood and waved him over.

One advantage of owning a restaurant was obviously that you got to enjoy the best table and service, even at the busiest time of day.

Quinn took a deep breath and made his way over to them. They'd saved a chair for him at the end of the blue-painted planks that made up the table. There wasn't much trust to be found in any of the unusual gray eyes that stared back at him.

"Where's Selena? I thought she was coming, too." She had been the closest he had to an ally.

"As she sits on the commission, she didn't want any hint of impropriety, so she thought it best if she stayed out of it. She plays by the rules." Xavier poured a tall glass of iced lemonade. "What did you want to talk about?"

"If we work together, we can find a solution to keep the land in your family and the ranch working."

Belle crossed her arms over the table and narrowed her eyes at him. "How?"

"Working with the city, county and state, along with some other international organizations, the land can be put in a trust and then zoned to protect the endangered ocelots and sea turtles."

She leaned back, her face closed off. "How does that help us support the ranch and give us the funds to continue supporting the displaced people rescued by Xavier's group?"

"That's the detail we need to work out. What I'm proposing is that the Foundation lease the land that runs along the coast on a long-standing basis. We've never done this kind of project before. I'm hoping we can establish a nonprofit branch specifically for this project. It would be a separate organization that would focus on long-term research while protecting the wildlife habitats along this shoreline. The sea turtles and ocelots will have a protected piece of coastal land where scientists can study them. We'd pay for the right to use the land."

"If it can be developed, we'll get enough to support

the rest of the ranch. How does this plan do that?" Elijah asked.

"It would take a little more time, and you wouldn't receive as much cash, but between grants and endowments, we could set up a trust. After an up-front lump sum, we would pay a lease. You would still own the land, and it would earn money on a monthly or quarterly basis. If handled carefully, it could also work as an educational site that brings in a certain type of tourist."

"How much are we talking?" Now it was Xavier's turn to stare him down.

Taking one of his business cards out of his breast pocket, Quinn wrote a few numbers on the back. "From the preliminary information our lawyer gave me, we could pay a larger amount quarterly than monthly because we'd be able to collect interest on the principle. It wouldn't be the huge amount you'd get from a developer, but it would be fair."

He wrote down the larger amount for the up-front payment, then slid the card over to Belle. "We can negotiate amounts once we get more details, but that's the up-front amount. And you'd keep any money that came from the other visitors. But we'd need to do a study on traffic and impact to certain areas to ensure the protection of the habitat."

Belle kept her head lowered as her fingers worked the edge of the little rectangle. There was not a single hint of emotion on her face. He had no clue what was running through her mind.

"Belle?" Reaching out, he stilled her fingers. "What are you thinking?"

"I need to talk with the boys." She glanced at the two men sitting across from her. "Damian needs to be in on

this, too. He's the one with the most legal knowledge."
Handing the card to Xavier, she sighed. "It's too good
to be true. What do you think? Would this be enough
to do what we want to help your people?"

Xavier's gaze swung between her and Quinn. "I don't
want Belle to get hurt. Could this work?" He turned
back to Belle. "Would you be okay with this? It's not
as much as if we sold, but it also keeps the land and the
ranch in the family, along with giving us extra income.
I can also investigate other sources of funding for our
project. Along with our other businesses, this might be
a good option." He shrugged. "I don't know enough to
say one way or another yet."

Quinn waited. She avoided his gaze, staring out over
the water.

Elijah swirled his chip in the salsa. "It ties up the
land for a long time. Are you okay with that, Belle?"

She popped her knuckles, her shoulders weighted
down. He had wanted to lighten her burden, not give
her another hard decision.

Quinn nodded. "That's the point as far as the
Foundation's goals are concerned. We don't want it developed, but I don't want to hurt the family ranch, either.
We can both win if we come together on this. This is
not anywhere near a done deal. It's an option I want to
give you. I'm also open to other ideas you might have.
We have less than a month to move forward and get
more details."

Shaking her head, she looked at the card. "Why are
you doing this?"

"Because you're a fighter and the fight should be
fair." He leaned forward but kept his hands from touch-
ing hers. "I want you to win."

He wanted to be her champion and roar into battle for her, but that would be wrong on so many levels. Trust didn't come easy to her. How could it with the way her mother, uncle and others abandoned and abused her.

"I'm not asking for a commitment. Just the chance to work with you to see if it can be a win for all of us. Will you give me a chance?"

With a glance at the other two men, she nodded. "Okay. But I want you to know that I don't trust any of this. We need to speak with Damian, and I'll have our lawyers look at everything."

"Of course." Tension that he hadn't even been aware of left his shoulders.

A cavalry charge came from Elijah's pocket. "Jazz." He smiled, then answered the phone. "Hey, babe. Yeah, we're done. It went well." He stood and walked away from them.

Quinn stole a peek at Belle to see if she had any problems with that statement. Her face was still neutral. "Belle. I didn't set out to trick you." He sighed. "I never meant to make you feel like I was spying on you."

She adjusted the clip holding her hair. "Okay. So, it's all just weird timing?"

"It was. I didn't even know you were the 4-H horse person. Of course, we wouldn't have been in Port Del Mar if I wasn't gathering information. Not just your ranch, but the whole area is critical to the survival of several species. Your location just happens to be the best location that is still undeveloped."

She nodded but didn't say another word. Her focus stayed on the rolling waves. Xavier twisted his mouth, then shrugged as he spoke. "It does all seem too convenient. Being at the horse club meeting when your house is struck by lightning. Finding the ocelots. The kids becoming friends. Using your kids to infiltrate our family."

"What? You think—"

She threw her wadded napkin at Xavier. "He's messing with you. Ignore him."

Xavier winked at him.

Quinn grinned at his own gullibility. He had always wanted siblings, the camaraderie that came from growing up with people. They had a closeness he envied. The closest he had ever come to that was with Kari.

For a second, he closed his eyes. The familiar images of Kari morphed into Belle. Talk of Diamondback swirled around them. Belle laughed at a joke Xavier made. Even when life was hard, they had each other.

They didn't notice the turbulence he was going through. This was the reason he and Kari had wanted a big family.

Being only children was something they had both shared. She should be here, helping to raise their children and filling their lives with childhood memories.

Elijah came back to the table, still on the phone. "Okay. Yes. I'll let him know." A few more words, then he put the phone away. "Selena and Jazz wanted to make sure you knew to come to Xavier and Selena's house Saturday. It's an Easter prep party."

Belle made a small distressed sound. Not good.

"What's that?" Quinn asked.

Elijah looked confused. "An Easter prep party is where you make stuff for Easter."

Quinn snorted. "Yeah, I get that, but what are you prepping? Do you dye eggs? The girls have done that a couple of times." Had Jonah? He couldn't remember.

Belle answered, "We don't just soak the eggs in color. There are all sorts of ways to decorate an egg. We also build our piñata and create the paper flowers we'll put at the cross after church. The best part is making dozens of *cascarones* to hide."

He was sure Belle didn't want him crashing her family get-together. "Tell her thank you, but we can't make it."

Elijah creased his brow. "You have another social engagement? Jazz and Selena come across all sweet and nice, but they are undercover dictators. They weren't asking."

"They're good at telling others what they should be doing. It's easier to go along with it—and they're usually right, anyway." Belle finally turned her gaze to him. "You should let the kids come. They'll have a great time. It's a family tradition we do every year."

"Family traditions?" Not his family, though.

"My kids want your kids there." She gave him a tentative smile. Not the one he had come to look forward to.

He hadn't realized how much he'd missed her smile. Not that it mattered. Soon he'd be in another part of the world. "Gina can bring the kids." He paused. "They actually make the *cascarones*? Is it safe?"

"Yes. The eggshells have been disinfected before they stuff the confetti inside. And they have no problem cracking them over anyone's head they can reach."

Xavier laughed. "Coating everyone's hair with dots of color might be their favorite part of Easter. The bigger the mess, the better. Selena said she invited you the other day when she saw you at the multiples group thing."

"She did, but I didn't want to intrude. And I wasn't sure what it was we were being invited to."

Belle gave him another forced smile. "Your kids are always welcome."

He shouldn't be disappointed that she didn't include him. It wasn't like he was ever going to be in a relationship with her.

He needed to stay focused on his job. Now he had new details to work out if he was going to make everyone happy before he left. Soon he'd be planning the next project. Then, before the weather cooled, they would be gone. Off to a new country.

Normally, that was the exciting part of the job for him. Maybe he was getting old. The thought of moving to another country just made him tired.

Chapter Thirteen

Belle took the box full of colorful tissue paper and silk flowers from the trunk of Jazz's car. "Is this the last of it?"

Her sister-in-law nodded. "I have the rest in the backyard. The tables are set up."

Cassie ran across the yard, Lucy and Rosie close behind. "Mom. Do y'all need help? Can we start making the piñata?"

The other two girls jumped and clapped, their excitement bubbling over.

"We should wait for the twins and Jonah. They're coming, right?" Lucy asked.

Jazz closed the back of her SUV. "They should be here any minute. Let's get this to the back. I've got snacks." They ran to the deep wraparound porch and disappeared into the large Victorian home.

At the side gate, Belle turned to open the latch. A gust of wind took the top layers of tissue. Dropping the box to save them, she was running them down when Quinn arrived. His kids tumbled out of the car, giggling as they chased across the lawn to help her gather the escaped paper.

Buelita, Selena's great-grandmother, sat on the porch and laughed at their antics as she twisted stems for the paper roses. Belle's girls and Rosie came through the back gate to join the chaos. Quinn and his mother-in-law climbed out of his Land Rover and Gina made her way to sit with Buelita while Quinn grabbed the sheets that had gone into the street.

He brought the orange and yellow paper to her. "A game of chase with tissue paper is not what I envisioned for your Easter prep party."

"It's the most popular game. It's trending, you know." She looked up from the stack of paper and met his direct gaze.

Her breath caught in her throat. His stare went to the depths of her bones.

She didn't want to feel the loss of possibilities when she saw him. She'd been fine without a man in her life. Not only had she survived, but she and her girls had flourished.

So why was she so upset at the thought of never knowing what it would be like to be his?

They had corresponded through email since the court hearing, but she still wasn't sure that the plan he'd mapped out would work or why he was doing this.

"I'm glad you decided to bring the kids. You'll have fun." She turned from him as the kids surrounded them, chatty and laughing as they handed off the rainbow of craft paper that had littered the front yard.

See, Belle, you can be normal around him. Or at least act like her heart wasn't pounding in her ears.

"I'm not staying. I promised the kids they could come,

and Gina wanted to visit with Buelita, but I have work to do. I'll be home in a few hours."

All six kids ran to the porch and surrounded Buelita and Gina. They were all calling Gina "Baba" now, just like they all called Selena's great-grandmother by her "Buelita" title.

Buelita was the closest her girls had to a grandmother, and now they had adopted Gina, too.

The two older women laughed at something. Jonah, the only boy in the group, had climbed into his grandmother's lap.

Keeping her gaze on the happy generations on the porch, Belle avoided looking at Quinn again. "You have to work on a Saturday?" she asked. "Does it have to do with the Diamondback?"

"No. It's our project in South America. It's the next place we'll be going, and we're lining up our contacts and scoping out locations to stay."

She knew he was leaving. She knew. "You move a lot. What's the longest you've stayed anywhere?"

"Most stays are six to seven months. A few are shorter, only a month or so. The longest has been nine months. Our base is in Houston, so I have a town house there." They fell silent. "I've got to go. I'll be back later." He waved to his kids, then carefully covered his eyes with dark shades before going toward his car.

Taking a moment, Belle watched him walk across the lawn. His confident stride owned the ground he walked on. It was good that he was leaving. She made herself turn away from him. She needed time on her own to learn to breathe again. Heading to the side gate for the second time, she made a list of all the reasons she should not be in a relationship.

Balancing the box on one hip, she struggled to open the gate without losing any of the tissue this time. It couldn't be done, so she had to set them down.

"Belle." His smooth, deep voice interrupted her thoughts and caused her to jump.

He moved closer to her. With both hands he removed his sunglasses. "There's something that's been bothering me, and we need to talk. You've been avoiding me. With everything that's happened, I know it's difficult to trust me. I want you to know that it's okay if you question everything I do—but give me a chance to prove to you that I want the best for you and your family."

She bit her lip. "I'm sorry, but I can't trust anyone with my family. It's not personal." A yearning to step into his arms and give him everything was dangerously close to the surface, but she knew better. "I'll listen when it comes to the plan you have for the coastline, but I can't let you in my life. You'll be gone soon. Your kids might be used to leaving friends, but that's not easy for my girls or for me."

Sadness clouded his clear eyes. "I wish it could be different, but I understand. I miss your friendship."

"You're leaving soon, so it doesn't make much of a difference."

His gaze searched her face. She wanted to hide, but she kept her chin high. Then he nodded. "I get it. I'll see you later." With his hands in his pockets and his shoulders down, he went to his car again.

The sheriff pulled up. He walked straight to her, waving for Quinn to join them. Buelita disappeared into the house and, a few minutes later, returned with Xavier and Elijah, who stepped off the porch to join them.

Cantu shook hands with everyone. "I came to speak with Xavier, but I'm glad you're all here."

Elijah crossed his arms. "What's up? Is it our mother or the rustlers?"

Belle prayed it wasn't something new.

"Both. We finally got two of your cattle thieves to admit who sent them. It was Randy Anderson and your mother."

Okay. That was not what she had been expecting. "Our mother was stealing our cattle?"

Elijah swung around and looked to the sky. "That's a new low."

"They said she told them you owed her, and she was just taking what you had denied her."

"You don't believe her, do you? She doesn't have a right to those cattle." She turned to Elijah. "She had set this up before she even talked to us. Where is she now?"

"We picked her up. She's saying that it's a mis-understanding and that she is part owner of the ranch. Are you pressing charges, or is this a family matter?"

Xavier scowled. "We're pressing charges. She doesn't have any—"

Quinn held up a hand. "You might be able to use this in your favor."

They all looked at him.

"How much time do we have?" Quinn asked Cantu.

"We could release her but tell her to stay in town."

They discussed options for a few more minutes. Then the sheriff left.

Xavier grunted. "That woman is unbelievable. I'm going to make some phone calls to some buddies of mine that can help. Thanks, Quinn." He left with Elijah.

Quinn moved closer to Belle as if to hold her, but his

arms dropped, and he shrugged. "I know it hurts that she did this, but it might work in our favor."

"Thanks. I've got to get these to the party." She didn't want to talk to anyone.

"I'll see you later." He put his sunglasses back on and walked away from her again.

"Mijo!" Buelita called to him from the porch, before he could reach the sidewalk.

Belle escaped to the backyard. They had a party to prepare. That was what her mind needed to be focused on today. Not on all the what-could-have-beens if life had been different. It wasn't, and it wasn't going to be.

"Mijo, come sit." The older woman who had fast become Gina's friend patted the empty spot next to her on the large porch swing. "Where are you running off to? Your family is here. You need to relax. I'm old and can see those lines on your face. Stay and play. Take it from me, those babies will grow up *mucho* fast."

There was no way he was going to tell her that the real problem was being so close to Belle. That she made him forget who he was and his goals. He sighed, not sure how to explain.

His mother-in-law lowered her chin and looked at him over the top of her glasses. "Stop hiding. Your children need you to be fully present in your life."

Both women stared him down and there was nothing to say. The only options left to him were to nod and go to the gate Belle had gone through.

When he stopped at the corner of the Victorian, a backyard full of family, music and laughter—and a huge mess of color scattered over several tables—greeted him.

His attention went straight to the middle table. Belle was smiling with a brightness he hadn't seen lately. She was surrounded by all the kids as they made the confetti eggs that would end up being smashed over people's heads.

Her eyes met his, and she froze. The beautiful smile fell, and she straightened.

His children squealed and ran over to him, throwing their arms around him. "You stayed." Hannah took his hand and led him to the table where Belle sat. Selena announced that she had the frame ready to make the piñata at the last table.

Meg patted the bench. "Sit here, Daddy, and help them finish. We told Ms. Selena we'd help make the piñata. It's a giant Easter egg and it'll be full of candy and prizes." The twins took off, but Jonah climbed up next to Lucy.

Quinn studied Belle from behind the safety of his dark sunglasses. Tension held her shoulders tight. She had been having fun until he stepped into the backyard. "Sorry to crash your party, but when I get double-teamed by the grandmothers, there's no saying no."

She had to grin at that. "This is for the kids, anyway, right?"

"Right." He surveyed the backyard and found pockets of chaos as everyone got involved in a variety of activities. "My kids have never done anything like this. We've participated in local church Easter egg hunts. When the girls were small, they dyed eggs with their mom. Thank you for including them."

"It was Selena's idea. Her dad, Riff, was a musician." She nodded to the group playing various sorts of instruments. "She traveled a great deal as a kid, and she's sensitive to children needing traditions. Your kids are great. Mine would never have let me hear the end of it if we didn't invite them."

On the table where his twins were seated, Selena had placed a bamboo structure in the shape of an egg. The girls were already covered in runny glue as they layered strips of newspaper over it.

The back door opened, and the grandmothers went straight to the table piled high with flowers and more tissue paper of every imaginable color.

"Y'all must go through a ton of tissue paper."

"We stockpile it." The corner of her mouth flicked up. "Have you made *cascarones* before?"

Swinging his leg over the bench, he shook his head.

"It's fun, Daddy." Pieces of pink and yellow paper stuck to his son's hair. Bath time was going to be interesting tonight. Jonah put drops of glue on top of an egg, then pressed a precut square over the hole. He lifted it and smiled at him.

One of his front teeth didn't look right. Quinn leaned closer. Was his son about to lose his first baby tooth?

Lucy held her egg up, too. "I have one, too. I showed him how to put the glue on. Just a dot…" Her small hand lifted the cotton swab with glue and gently touched another spot. "A hop and a dot. I've been helping since I was little. Right, Mama?"

"Yes, you have, and you did a great job of showing Jonah and his sisters how to make them."

"Jonah, let's go make flowers. Mama, can we?" With a nod from Belle, they scrambled off the bench and ran to the grandmothers.

"Quinn, if you want, I'll show you how it's done."

She looked over her shoulder. "Or you can join the men at the pit."

Elijah and Xavier were standing next to a brick firepit. A delicious aroma wafted through the air. There were a few people he recognized at other tables. "Wow. This is just the prep party? I can't imagine what the actual day will look like. Y'all take this seriously." This was the kind of family tradition his kids were missing.

"This is nothing compared to Christmas. Wait until you see us in action for that. The whole town turns into a winter wonderland. The kids are going to—" She clamped her mouth shut and looked away. "Sorry. Y'all won't be here."

Silence fell hard between them.

She sighed. "Do you know when you'll be leaving?"

"I'd planned to leave at the end of the month, but with the change of plans, we're reworking all the strategies and reports, so it looks like it's going to take a few months. Grants take time, and there are several we'll need to get this started."

"I'm not so sure that's even possible."

"I promise, I won't leave until we're all happy with the results. This new development with your mother might prove to be the leverage we need to take her out of the equation. The girls asked if they could stay through the summer, and we'll need the time. It'll work out."

"If they're going to be here, that'll be great. We have a horse-judging event next month in Austin. I hope they can go. Both of your girls bring so much to the team. Not only do they know the anatomy and conformation of a horse, they're articulate beyond their years when it comes to explaining their answers. They're impressive. Which makes sense with both parents being scientists."

"Kari's father was a scientist, too. It's in their blood. Me being involved is an accident. I liked the ocean and didn't know what else to do until I met her. What a man will do for love, right?" Which was why he had to stay focused on his goal. It was for Kari.

She looked down. "An accident? Don't sell yourself short. You know what you're doing, and your passion for the environment shows." With a glance at the kids, she sighed. "You're a good man and father. I imagine that, if she were here, she would say you were a good husband, too. In my experience, most men expect their wives to give in to what they want, no matter their own dreams. Her dreams became yours. Some husbands find it easier to destroy dreams."

He groaned. Her husband. *Okay, it's official. Quinn, you're an idiot around her.* "He didn't deserve you." He kept his voice low as he leaned in close to her.

A sad smile lifted the edges of her lips. "That's true. But I have two beautiful girls that I wouldn't trade for the world. And lessons that will last a lifetime." She shifted and looked over his shoulder, as if seeking an escape. "Sounds like you'll leave in August."

"End of July is what we're shooting for. If we stay later, I'm afraid the girls will be asking to start school with their friends. Homeschooling is so much easier with the travel."

"With all the places y'all go, I imagine their education is better than anything a school can offer." Her head jerked to him. "What'll happen to the ocelots when you leave?"

"They're getting older, so I'll turn them over to the local wildlife preserve. They'll prep them for release. Hopefully, back here on the ranch if it all works out."

She nodded. They stood, watching their families.

"Belle, I appreciate everything you've done for us. I know the kids will have great memories of Port Del Mar and the Diamondback Ranch." His throat closed. He'd have his own memories and regrets.

"Childhood memories should be happy." Hands stuffed in her pockets, she rocked on the heels of her boots. "What will—"

A cry from the flower table had them both running. Jonah was crying.

Quinn went down on his knees in front of his son. "What happened? Are you okay?"

Blood spattered Jonah's face, hand and shirt, but he couldn't tell where it was coming from. He glanced at Gina. The color had left her face.

She shook her head. "I don't know. He cried out and blood was on his hands. He wouldn't tell me what was wrong. Is he bleeding from the mouth?"

"Cassie, go get the first-aid kit." Belle sent her daughter to the house as everyone gathered around to offer help.

Jonah had one hand over his mouth and the other in a tight fist against his stomach. Gently, Quinn tried to remove his son's hand from his face.

"Can you tell me what's wrong?" Hand lowered, the boy shook his head. He had his lips pressed closed. Quinn tried to pick up his other hand, and the boy cried out.

A gap was front and center. Holding Jonah's chin, he tried to get a better look. Relief eased his muscles. "It's your tooth."

Cassie returned with the first-aid kit and handed it to her mother. Belle opened it and handed him a wipe to clear the blood. "He lost a tooth. Is it his first time?"

A muffled sob came from Jonah. "I didn't lose it." He opened his other hand to show them his tooth. "I was eating candy, and it broke in my mouth. I'm sorry, Daddy. I didn't mean to do it. It won't go back. I tried."

Quinn sat next to him and pulled him into his lap. "You didn't break it. It's a baby tooth, and you're not a baby anymore, so your teeth will be falling out now to make room for your adult ones." He used the washcloth Belle gave him to clean the blood.

"I'm not in trouble?" A hiccup had Jonah's little chest heaving.

The gathering adults congratulated him before moving back to what they had been doing. Gina moved next to him and whispered words that soothed him. "You're such a big boy now."

He nodded and showed her the hole where his front tooth had been. "I don't need my baby teeth anymore, Baba. That's what Daddy said." Doubt edged his words. "Will they all fall out? How will I eat?"

Belle knelt at Quinn's knee and smoothed Jonah's silky hair off his face. "We have some clean T-shirts inside that would fit you. Do you want one?" She gazed up at Quinn, and for a moment he was locked in her eyes. Then she blinked and went back to his son.

Jonah slipped an arm around her neck, slipping off his father's lap into her arms. Laying his head on her shoulder, he closed his eyes. Leftover hiccups from crying disrupted his breathing. Soothing him, Belle stood and moved toward the house, Lucy close behind.

Quinn followed. He wasn't sure what he was doing, but it was better than feeling completely useless.

Chapter Fourteen

Belle handed Jonah a mirror. With a clean shirt and washed face, he sat on the edge of the island in the middle of the huge country kitchen. The smell of fresh baked goods made Belle's mouth water.

Selena's kitchen always smelled so good. Buelita's mission in life was to feed everyone, and she was good at it.

Jonah pulled his lips back and examined his new gap. "Do I sound funny?"

The girls laughed. "You haf a wisp now," Hannah said, then giggled.

"Hannah." Quinn glared at her. "You're fine, Jonah. Before you know it, your new tooth will be in and it will all even out. The girls had no front teeth at all when you were born."

"Really?" All three looked at him.

He looked a little surprised at first. Then he grinned. "I'd forgotten that."

The window over the sink had his full attention, and he looked a little lost. Maybe it was the memories. That time in their lives had to be hard on him.

Belle stepped up and patted Jonah's knee. "See, they have great teeth now. You'd never know they were toothless. I'm sure they sounded a little different then, too."

"They did. It sounded as if they were whistling half the time." Quinn hugged the girls to either side of him. "It's time for us to head home."

"But we're making the piñata," both the girls said at once.

Belle intervened. "Why don't you and Jonah spend some father-son time celebrating this milestone? Losing your first baby tooth is a big deal. I can bring the girls with me."

"Please, please, Daddy?" They pressed their hands together, practically bouncing on their feet.

"How about it, Jonah? Just you and me? We could get some ice cream at the pier and watch the boats."

"Yes!" He reached for his father. "The twins said Mama loved boats."

"She did. Know what else she loved?"

The little boy frowned. "Ice cream?"

"No, silly." Quinn tickled his little tummy. "You. She loved you so much."

"But she didn't know me. That's what Hannah and Meg said."

A knot lodged in Belle's throat. There was such sadness in Quinn's eyes. Stepping up, she put her hand on Jonah's back. "Moms know their babies from the moment they know you are on your way. She talked to you and laughed when you kicked her." She searched Quinn's face. She didn't want to say the wrong thing, but this little boy needed to know his mother had loved him. "She helped pick out your name."

Quinn nodded, took a deep breath and hugged his

son close. "She knew your name the minute we heard your heartbeat. She's the one who bought you Buck, because she knew you would love horses. We had little tiny pictures of you before you were born, and she carried them with her to show everyone her son. She held you for as long as she could, but then she had to go. She made me promise to tell you every day that I love you. I should have told you that she loves you, too."

Belle's heart was breaking. She didn't understand so much of this world, but she knew this man was the kind of father her uncle and ex would never understand. He deserved a woman who could give him one hundred percent without holding back.

He looked at Belle, and her heart rolled over.

No, he was not for her. She was too much of a De La Rosa. All they did was hurt people in the long run. Elijah and Xavier cherished their wives and were devoted husbands now, but it hadn't been easy. She couldn't risk putting her girls through the trauma of a breakup.

"Are you sure about the girls?" he asked.

All she could manage was a nod and a half-baked smile.

"Good. Thank you. We need some one-on-one time." He swung Jonah over his head and they headed out, echoes of little-boy giggles warming her heart.

It had been a few hours, but she could still hear Jonah's and Quinn's laughter as they had headed out for their male bonding time. He was such a good father. It made sense that he and his wife had wanted a houseful of kids.

She washed the last of the dishes, letting her mind wander. Which was dangerous. It went places it shouldn't.

Like to her and Quinn in a huge house like Xavier and Selena's with kids in every room.

"Oh, she has it bad. Look at that expression." Jazz's voice pulled her out of her musings.

"I know it has nothing to do with those dishes," Selena teased.

She needed to stop this before it even started. "You both need to stop. There is nothing between us and there never will be."

"Because you're being stubborn."

Jazz nodded. "He likes you. A lot."

They didn't get that she was not his type. He'd never want someone like her. "We're friends. I don't have a lot of those. I don't want to lose his friendship. If we tried to make it more, there would be expectations and… stuff. I don't do emotions or relationship things well."

They both laughed. "You're a De La Rosa. It might not come easy, but if Elijah and Xavier can figure it out, so can you."

"You're afraid of the unknown." Jazz sat on a bar stool and propped her feet up.

With a snort, Belle shook her head. "Oh, no. Being married is not the unknown. I'm very much afraid of what I do know. We'd be better as just friends. He's happy traveling."

Jazz arched her back. "You De La Rosas are the most hardheaded people I know. Elijah tried to feed me the same line." She made a face and lowered her voice. "'We're better off with miles between us.'" She rolled her eyes. "He actually said that and believed it."

She had both women's full attention. "What did you do to get him to change his mind?" Selena asked.

"I left."

They all laughed.

One hand rubbing her baby bump, Jazz sighed. "I also left it up to God. Everyone talked to Elijah, including my mother. God had to work double time to get through that hard head of his. I knew I couldn't force him. That's what got us in trouble the first time around."

Selena smiled. "And now we have another De La Rosa on the way." She turned to Belle. "You deserve a happy ending, too. Quinn could be it. If you're willing to let your guard down and trust him."

Tears burned Belle's eyes. "He'll be halfway around the world. Not that it matters. I don't have enough to give him."

Selena came to her side at once. "Sweetheart, you have so much to give. Why not at least try? You're a beautiful woman. All you do is work. Give yourself permission to have fun."

"What if he wants more?" She knew it sounded lame, but she couldn't help that fear from playing havoc with her self-confidence.

Jazz wrapped an arm around her. "It's not an all-or-nothing kind of thing. He's a nice guy. Why don't you deserve a little happiness?"

She moved away from them. "I want Quinn to leave so my life can return to normal. Relationships are not for me."

Both women looked at her as if she had claimed a burning bush talked to her. Rolling her eyes, she turned to put away the last of the dried dishes. "Just because you two are gooey in love doesn't mean I need to be. I'm perfectly happy with my life as it is. Once we get my mother out of town and Quinn on his way, life will go back to the way it was before and I'll be a very happy cowgirl."

They both shook their heads as if they didn't believe a word she said. Truth be told, she was a bit worried that, even after Quinn left, she would never be the same as she was before.

Knowing him had changed her. But the jury was still out on whether that was a good thing or not.

Tonight was his turn to read to the kids. They were halfway through a collection of children's Bible stories. The girls remained quiet, letting Jonah answer the last question at the end of the story.

With each other, they were competitive, but they were also good about allowing their little brother time to shine. Jonah snuggled between them again, his new Buck tucked against his side.

He'd told his sisters again how their mother had bought it for him before he was born. They went on to tell him stories of how they had helped their mom get ready for him. Quinn wasn't sure if they came from their own memories, or if they had been told the stories and seen the pictures.

Gina was good about sharing pictures of their mother with them. Closing the book, he stood, leaned over and kissed each of them on the forehead.

"Daddy?" Hannah turned to him.

"Um?" The night was quiet as his little birds nested in their blankets.

"You should marry Ms. Belle." All three of his little birds looked up at him and nodded.

"We could be a real family," Meg added.

He sat again. "We are a real family."

"But it would be great. You like her. She likes you," Hannah answered.

"We like Cassie and Lucy. They like us. We'd make a super awesome family," Meg continued, without missing a beat.

Jonah sat up. "We could all live at the ranch and be happy."

That made his heart twist. "You're not happy?"

All three said, "We are."

Meg looked at her siblings. "But we can always be happier."

Tucking the comforter around them, he gave them one last kiss. "Stop plotting my love life and go to sleep." He turned off the reading lamp and went downstairs. If he stayed right now, they would probably keep talking.

Gina was standing at the small stove making tea. With a heavy thud, he fell into what had become his favorite chair. Would Belle let him take it with him? He'd never had a favorite chair before.

Gina handed him the warm tea in one of her new, delicate cups.

"Thanks."

"They're right, you know. She makes you happy. I love that you've started whistling and singing again."

Leaning his head back, he closed his eyes. He was starting to see that.

"My daughter, your wife, would never have wanted you to stop living or to turn your back on God. I realized something recently. We have both blamed ourselves for her death, but it wasn't our fault. It was just one of those things we won't understand while we're here on Earth. You know it wasn't your fault?"

He leaned forward and braced his elbows on his knees. "I know."

"Kari would want you to love again. It doesn't take anything away from her or the love you will always have for her. That will always be in your children."

Unable to speak, he nodded.

She sipped her tea. "What are you going to do about it?"

"Do you want to stay in Port Del Mar?" This would be a huge step. Could he take it?

"I would be very happy here. But I would also be happy wherever you and the children are. Son, don't do this for me. Or them. If we stay, do it because it's what God has led you to do."

This was the first time in over five years he felt like he wanted a home. Maybe it was time to consider making it permanent.

But first, he needed to make sure that everything with the land was settled.

He needed to make this right.

Chapter Fifteen

Two days later, Belle stopped at the doorway. The kitchen was a mess. Cassie stood at the island, one of Mari's aprons double wrapped around her waist as she mixed something in a bowl. Banana peels and bits of apple littered the counter.

"Hurry, Lucy. Mama will be back anytime, and I want the kitchen clean." Cassie stuffed what looked like a peanut butter mix into pitas. Were the girls trying to surprise her with dinner?

A grin pulled at her lips as she scanned the area for her youngest daughter. A sound came from the pantry. The door was open, blocking Belle's view. Then it moved, and a chair wobbled.

Her heartbeat pummeled her ears as she rushed to prevent a worst-case scenario. Belle had Lucy in her arms as the chair tipped over, a large bag of chips clutched in her little hands.

"Mama!" both girls yelled at the same time. She eased Lucy to the ground and turned to Cassie.

"What's going on, girls?"

Cassie took the chips from her sister. "Lu, are you okay?" Cassie hovered over her sister.

"She's fine. Why is my kitchen a mess?"

The girls looked at each other, then down. "Lucy?" Her youngest would cave faster.

Panic in her eyes, she turned to her sister.

"Lucy. Why are y'all fixing dinner without me?"

Cassie stepped forward. "Mr. Quinn called, and we invited them for dinner."

"What?" Heart racing, she turned to the kitchen.

She'd gotten so busy that it had been neglected. And now Quinn was coming over, and her house was not ready for guests.

Her hand went to her messy hair. Her breath came in quick, shallow pants. Last-minute surprises never went well. She needed…

Lucy grabbed her hand. "What is it, Mama?"

"We need to scrub the kitchen and get the dishes done and put away. There are toys and clothes scattered all over the living room. I need a shower. When will they be here?"

Cassie's eyes darted around the room, then back at her. Concern clouded her eyes. "Mama, we made dinner. You take a shower and get ready. Wear the yellow shirt. It's pretty. Lucy and I'll clean the house."

Sweat broke out over her skin, and her lungs refused to work. Closing her eyes, she bent over and braced her hands over her knees.

In. One. Two. Three. Hold. One. Two. Three. Out. One. Two. Three. Hold.

Several more breathing cycles helped to calm her. Both girls were watching her now, concern on their sweet little faces.

Lack of sleep had pushed her over the edge, and she was irrational. This was Quinn, not Frank or Jared. Smiling at the girls, she straightened. He would be fine with the dinner the girls had made.

"Let's set the table with the fancy plates. That will be fun." She went to the china cabinet and pulled out her aunt's favorite dishes. Half of the delicate dishes with tiny violet flowers and pretty green vines had been broken years ago—and it had been her fault.

Wanting to make her brother's birthday special like Mari had, she had set the table with them, but her uncle's temper exploded with her efforts. He'd thrown them across the room at her as he called her...

Lucy's voice brought her back to the present. "Mama, Jonah's dad is a really good dad. Just like Tío Eli and Tío Xavier. Don't you think so?"

Taking a deep breath, she looked at her youngest. Dots of bright yellow and purple, leftovers from the *cascarones* they'd brought home and finished the day before, surrounded her daughter at the table.

Unsure of the unpredictable direction of her daughter's thoughts, she nodded and waited.

Not looking up from her task, Lucy gathered a stack of empty egg cartons. She kept talking as she disappeared into the pantry. "Everyone at school has a dad. Julie's dad left, but she still sees him. She has a room in San Antonio when she stays with him."

Cassie gathered all the dishes and took them to the sink. "A dad would be nice, but not everyone has one. Sometimes dads aren't nice people, and it's good when they leave like ours did. Mom didn't have one, and we don't need one, either." She looked at her mom over her shoulder. "Right, Mom?"

Belle's throat went dry. "Families come in all different forms." And this was what she had dreaded. Her mother's heart ached. This was a void she couldn't fill in her daughters' lives. How did she explain that she didn't even have a name for the man who fathered her?

As a child, she'd grown to hate school events that involved parents. They left her feeling like an outsider.

The humiliation of feeling "less than" because they didn't have a good family was the one thing she never wanted her girls to experience.

"Jonah thinks you're a good mom. I told him you were the best. If we become a family, we'd have a dad and they'd get a mom. Not having a mom is worse than not having a dad. I feel bad for them."

Belle's mouth dropped open, but no words came to her mind. This was a minefield of issues.

Cassie leaned forward across the table. "Mama, it would be nice for you to have someone to help you." She looked down. "But we're good with just us, too."

"Jonah said he wished our mama could be his." Lucy cleaned the bananas and apples off the counter. "His is in heaven. He doesn't remember her. It would be great if you were their mother, and Mr. Quinn could be our father."

"Oh, baby. I can't just be his mother. He has a wonderful father and grandmother. There are lots of families that look different. It doesn't make us less of a family. As long as we love each other, we're good."

Lucy frowned. "They need a mom, and we need a dad. Why can't we move in together? We have room in our house."

"It doesn't work that way."

"Why not?" She was persistent; Belle had to give her that.

Cassie crossed her arms and frowned. "A mom and dad need to love one another to get married." She glanced at Belle. "You could love Mr. Quinn, right?"

Lucy frowned. "Did you love our daddy? Are you waiting for him to come back like Tío Xavier did?" Her eyes went wide. "And Tía Jazz! She came back to Tío Elijah. Where did our dad go?"

"No!" Cassie yelled at her sister. The dish towel was clenched in her fist, her face red. "We aren't waiting for him. He's mean. Mama sent him away so he wouldn't hurt us anymore."

Belle gasped. Had she not protected her girls as well as she thought?

Head down, Cassie jerked away from them and kept washing the dishes.

Lucy's eyes were wide. "He hurt us? I don't remember him. Mr. Quinn wouldn't hurt us. He's a good dad. Jonah said so."

Wanting to wrap both girls in her arms, Belle went to Lucy first. "Yes, Quinn's a good dad. Your father was…" She sighed, praying for the right words. "Some people have so much hurt and anger in them that it seeps over to other people. Your father was very angry at the world." She pulled Lucy into her arms. "We have God, and we have each other. We don't need anyone else. Girl power." She pressed her lips to her forehead. "I love you so much."

"I love you, too, Mama." The still-chubby arms went around her neck. "It doesn't matter how hurt or angry we get. It's not okay to hurt other people."

"That's right. I'm not going to let anyone hurt you."

Belle kissed her temple, and Lucy wiggled out of her arms to continue her task.

With her youngest settled, Belle approached Cassie. She put a hand on her shoulder. "He never…" Her heart was in her throat. Had she missed something? She'd been so diligent. "He never hurt you, did he?"

She shook her head. "No. But I saw him…hit you. And he yelled mean things."

Belle wrapped her arms around Cassie. She was growing so fast. "Nothing he said was true. The hate and loathing spewed out of him because it had nowhere else to go. I'm so sorry, baby."

"Why are you sorry? He…he's the sorry one." Her voice shook. She wiped her face. "Will you ever marry again? I mean, you don't need to, but it would be nice to have someone like Meg and Hannah's dad. He's really nice."

"Cassie."

"Never mind. Boys are stupid. We don't need a dad. Everything is good without one."

The yearning and loneliness in her daughter's voice pushed an ache so deep it went past her heart. Taking Cassie into a full hug, Belle pressed her cheek against the thick dark hair that smelled of the apple shampoo she'd used since she was a toddler. The other day, her daughter had asked for a new type of shampoo. A grown-up one.

"Not all boys are stupid. Your uncles are good men. They'd never hurt someone smaller or weaker than them."

Cassie hugged her tighter. "But they left you, Mama. You had to keep everything together when they couldn't. We don't need anyone else. Unless you like Mr. Quinn.

Do you want him to like you in that way…like a boy-friend?"

"No." Even to her own ears, that sounded sharp and a bit defensive. "No." Again, but calmer this time. "We're just friends, and we're working together to figure out a way to help the ranch and protect the coastline."

That had to be the reason he was coming. Had he gotten good news about the project? It was too soon. There were still a couple of months left. Or at least one. She hated surprises. Why not tell her?

Cassie put the dishes away. "Go take a shower, Mom. Lucy and I will finish. Right, Lucy?"

Lucy nodded and gave her a big smile, too big. "We've got this, Mama."

Deep breath. It was dinner with a friend. She'd won the hard-fought battle to control her own life, and she wasn't about to hand it over to him.

Quinn wasn't sticking around. In a few months— or sooner—he'd leave, and she could relax and go back to the way things were before he busted into her life.

She went to her room. He'd be gone soon, and all this internal turmoil would settle.

Quinn took the porch steps two at a time. Belle was going to be so excited about the news he had to share. It had happened so much faster than he had thought possible. God was smiling on them, and he couldn't wait to tell her.

He might even be more excited that she had invited him to dinner at her home. Just them, no other De La Rosas other than her girls. This was good.

His family gathered behind him as he knocked.

There was so much he wanted to share with her. Whistling, he knocked again.

"Are they in the barns?" Hannah asked, as they stood there for what seemed to be far too long.

He knocked again, a little harder this time. What if she had changed her mind? He looked at his phone. No texts.

Jonah was careful not to crush the bundle of sunflowers and larkspur they had picked out for Belle.

Since they were from the kids and not him, it would be easier for her to accept them. That was the plan, anyway.

Should they just walk in? In the morning they went straight to the barn from their cabin, then followed them into the house through the back. They'd never come through the front before.

The door opened. He blew out a breath he hadn't even been aware he was holding.

Cassie poked her head out and smiled. "Flowers!" She stepped back to let them into the house. "Mama's still getting ready."

"It was nice of your mother to invite us to dinner."

All five children giggled. "What's funny?" He eyed the kids. He had a feeling they were up to something.

Cassie glanced to the hallway, then to him. Her fingers were interlaced in a tight knot. "Let me get Mama."

Lucy waved them into the kitchen. There were candles and fancy dishes on the table set for seven.

Seven was a nice number. He watched as their kids worked together to get the dinner ready. Pitas stuffed with peanut butter, apples and bananas. "Your mom made this?"

"Nope. Cassie and I did. We've been helping Mama

more around the house. There's a lot to do, and the more help, the easier everything is."

Meg nodded. "When we all do a part, it is more fun, too."

The kids chatted, and he leaned on the counter to listen. This was what he wanted every day with Belle. Raising their children together as one family. Jonah made a strange noise, and before Quinn could tell him to stop, he had seized an empty pita in each hand like they were puppets. The girls were laughing so hard he didn't want to break it up.

That kid had the weirdest sense of humor. He was also getting too old to play with food.

"What's going on?" Belle stood in the doorway.

They all froze. Jonah snapped his hands behind his back, attempting to hide the now mangled bread pockets.

Quinn stepped forward. "The kids were putting the finishing touches on dinner. Thank you so much for inviting us over. It's great timing. I've got news I can't wait to share."

She glanced at her girls, then toward the flowers at the center of the table. "Those are pretty. But I think we've been played."

Narrowing his eyes, he studied the now very guilty-looking kids. "I was told you called and wanted us to join you for dinner."

Meg nudged Jonah.

"I'm sorry." Jonah smiled tentatively and held up the pitas to Belle.

Lucy stepped next to him. "Mama. He's so funny. He had one pita speaking Spanish, and the other was speaking Japanese, and they couldn't understand each other, so he was translating but getting it mixed up."

"My bread speaks Spanish and Japanese?" Hand on her chest, Belle eyed the basket of bread wrapped in a white-and-red kitchen towel. "Do any of my food speak English?"

Serious as could be, Jonah shook his head. "No. A little German, but not very well."

Quinn had to bite back a snort. "Baba is introducing German to their lessons. I'm so sorry, Belle. We can leave."

"No. No. No. The girls made dinner. It's not fancy, but it's one of their favorites. Where is Baba?"

"She's having a girls' night out with Buelita and a few of the ladies from the church," Hannah answered. "She said she'd stop by later for dessert."

With a smile that made him want more, she knelt in front of his son. Slowly, her tanned hands cupped his small ones, which were still holding the bread. "It looks as if the bread will now be visiting the barn. Do you make a habit of turning dinner into entertainment?"

Hannah and Meg gasped. "No, ma'am. Jonah, tell her you're sorry, and you won't do it again."

He frowned. "I am sorry, but I don't know if I'll not do it again. Sometimes my brain comes up with an idea, and my hands do it before I think about it."

"Jonah." Both girls sounded horrified at his confession.

Belle laughed. "It's called an impulse. As you get older, you'll learn to control it."

The boy's scowl deepened, and he looked at his dad. "That doesn't sound fun."

Meg crossed her arms. "It's called socially acceptable behavior. You want to be socially accepted, don't you?"

"Not if it's dull and boring."

Hannah's eyes narrowed. "You want Ms. Belle to like you?"

Horror crossed his face and his gaze swung to her. "I'm sorry. I promise to try to stop my impulse thinking. At least maybe not letting my hands do what my brain wants. I can't stop my brain from coming up with ideas." He looked at the bread. "I wasted good food that you made for us. I'm sorry." He looked like he was about to cry.

Belle pulled him close. "Oh, sweetheart. It's okay. All any of us can do is try to do better than the day before. On a positive note, the goats will love the special treat. You can take it to them later, after we eat. How does that sound?"

"It sounds okay if you still like me. Please don't get mad at Daddy. He does his best to teach me manners. I'm just not always very good at remembering. The girls are very good, though."

Lucy put an arm around him in solidarity. "I forget, too. That's why we have moms and dads."

Behind Belle, the twins were making motions for Jonah to hug her. Quinn narrowed his eyes. What were they up to? When Hannah noticed him watching, she elbowed her sister. They both stopped and tried to look innocent.

Jonah wrapped his arms around Belle, the bread still in his hands and now in her hair. She hugged him, then stood. "Come on. We'll put this in the scrap bucket. After dinner, the girls can take you out to feed the goats."

Like a faithful puppy, he followed her.

Quinn crossed his arms and pinned the girls with his best I-mean-business dad stare.

Cassie wrung her hands. "We want my mom to like Jonah."

Hannah's head bobbed at an overly fast rate. "You know how he can be, Daddy. He doesn't know how to act, and he annoys people."

"He's a little boy. When you were his age, you did the same things."

Both girls looked horrified. "We were not that bad."

"You told me we were invited to dinner, but Belle seems to think we invited ourselves."

Before the girls could answer, Belle and Jonah came back into the room, holding hands and speaking Spanish.

His heart took an extra jump. Belle met his gaze with a smile. Then she straightened, and her lips tightened. "Beautiful flowers and the best dishes on the table. *Qué pasa?*"

"Daddy has a surprise." Jonah probably didn't realize he was still speaking Spanish. Once he started one language, it was hard to get him to switch back. Jonah kept his hands in hers as he led her to the table. "I carried the flowers into the house and didn't crush one petal," he continued in Spanish.

"It's Spanish night?" Lucy clapped. She had also switched to Spanish.

Cassie sighed. "Does it have to be? English is so much easier."

"That's because you don't practice enough." Belle looked at Quinn. "Do you all speak Spanish enough to hold a conversation?" she asked in Spanish.

So he replied in kind. "*Sí.* Meg needs more practice, too." He smiled at the girls. "Like anything else, learning languages is easier for some than for others, but extra practice helps you gain confidence. It's okay to make mistakes."

There was some mumbling among the kids. Then they suddenly scrambled around the table, leaving two empty chairs next to each other. He rolled his eyes.

They really couldn't be more obvious.

But if they were on his side, it was all good.

As they sat, Belle leaned a little closer to him. "I love that you encourage different languages with your children. My ex didn't allow me to speak Spanish to the girls. He freaked if he heard anyone speaking Spanish. Cassie has a harder time, since she was older when he left."

He hadn't thought it was possible to like this guy less than he already did; he'd been wrong. "Why? It's part of your culture. And the more languages you speak, the more opportunities you have in the world."

"He wasn't a global type of guy, and he didn't want his kids to sound like…"

He waited for her to finish, but then again, he could imagine a few words the sad, sorry excuse for a man might have used. And they would be offensive in any language. Jared hadn't deserved Belle and her girls.

"Would you lead us in prayer?" Her soft voice brought him back to the table and the family sitting around him, holding hands and waiting.

They bowed their heads as he led them in prayer. Everything about this was good and right.

As soon as their hands dropped and they raised their heads, Belle turned to him. "So we were tricked into having dinner, but you said you had news?"

They all turned to him. He grinned and let the silence hang in the air for a moment.

She growled. "Quinn Sinclair."

With a laugh, he leaned in and grinned at her.

Her phone rang. She growled again, like a real growl from her chest. "It's Xavier. He never calls unless it's important." She put the phone to her ear. "Hey. What's up?"

Did she realize she was still speaking Spanish?

"Really?" She was silent for a long while, nodding her head as she listened. "That's more than fair." She nodded again. "Okay. Do you need anything from me?" She looked at Quinn and smiled. "Good. Once we get all the details, I'll do it. Thanks. Love you, too."

"My mom has agreed to the deal." Her grin went wider. "We'll have all charges dropped, and she'll sign over her part of the ranch to me. I'm going to meet with Jacoby to allow him to borrow my bull as restitution for his missing cattle." She sighed and leaned back, her face to the ceiling. "It's over. We're buying her out at a very manageable amount paid over the next year. She has signed over ownership of the ranch to me. Elijah didn't want it." There was a hint of moisture in her eyes when she looked at him. "I own a piece of the ranch now."

"That's awesome." He grinned as he took her hand and lightly squeezed. "Her stealing from you worked out."

"Yeah. I guess it did. I'm not sure I can take more, but you have to tell me your big news."

Shifting his weight forward on his elbows, he held her stare. "It came through. We have the first grant that is big enough to set up the endowment. The paperwork has been started. Two of the agencies we need to work with are on board. I have a great feeling about the rest. It looks as if we're going to be able to set everything up the way we want."

They all cheered. She bit her lip. "Are you sure?" Doubt was heavy in each word. "That was so much faster than you said."

"Yeah. I wasn't expecting it to go this smoothly. This is a gift. Your mother is out of the picture now. That was the one part I had no control over. It's all falling into place. Why do you look worried?"

All the kids sobered and stared at her. Smiling at them, she shook her head. "I'm in shock. Good news hasn't been knocking down my door lately. But this is a double blessing, so let's eat and give thanks for all of God's goodness."

The dishes were passed around and everyone talked. They laughed and teased each other. A few English words slipped in and they started a game of counting words. The one with the most words in English had to do the dishes. Cassie and Meg groaned.

A couple of times, Quinn had to remind Belle to eat. She was throwing questions at him faster than he could answer, and she still had a plate full of food when the kids had finished. There were warning signs that their restless children needed a new activity.

"Looks as if dinner is over and I lost." He slipped back to English. Meg and Cassie clapped and high-fived each other for not losing.

"Mom, since we're done, can we take the scraps to the goats?"

Belle stood. "Sure." Going to the door, she was blocked by Lucy.

"It's a celebration. We need ice cream."

Cassie nodded. "There are fresh strawberries in the fridge. Can you make the ice cream?"

"You make your own ice cream?" Quinn said. His kids were in awe.

Shrugging, Belle waved off their admiration. "We have an ice-cream maker. It's not that difficult." Facing the kids, she gave them a smile that lit up the room. "Y'all feed the goats and I'll get the ice cream going."

"I'll go with the kids now and do the cleanup when I return." He reluctantly stood to follow them.

"No!" all five voices cried out as one. Cassie shot a glare at the others. She gave them a look that was straight from Belle's game book. With a serene smile that resembled the cat in *Alice in Wonderland*, Cassie turned to them.

"Mom, why don't you show Mr. Quinn how we make the ice cream? It's fascinating. You don't have to worry about us. You can see the barn from the back porch. We want to play with the babies, so we'll be there awhile. A good while. You can help him wash the dishes." With that, she led her small group of mini matchmakers to the barn.

"Wait. I didn't use a single English word during dinner."

"Mom, he's a guest. Come on, guys. Let's go." She led her troops to the barn.

Hands on hips, Belle shook her head. "They couldn't be more obvious. Today, Lucy was going on about us becoming one family." She went into a large walk-in pantry at the end of the screened porch and returned with a tub-looking thing. "I can't believe our plan might work. Does this mean you'll be leaving sooner?"

His gaze went to the happy little troop running and

skipping to the barn. They stopped to inspect something on the ground before marching off again. "I'm glad we found a way to keep your family on the ranch. You've given your children a wonderful place to grow up."

All her attention was on the barrel-like appliance. "You've given your children the world. I mean, Jonah is only five—" she flipped her braid over her shoulder and stared at the kids making their way across the field "—and he speaks, like, four languages. Your girls are so self-assured and speak more like adults. Actually, better than most adults I know."

He'd been doing the dishes and finishing kitchen cleanup. Now he sat on the stool next to the rustic pine table. "Yeah, but there are drawbacks. Last weekend, Jonah told his Sunday school class that he needed prayer because we were homeless and had been his whole life. I'm not sure he sees all the traveling as a gift."

She stopped what she was doing and placed a hand on his arm. "Homeless? He doesn't really think that, does he?"

With a shrug, he sighed. The kids had gone into the barn. "He asked his class to pray for us to have a real home. Ann, the Sunday school teacher, let me know because she was worried and told me the church could help us if we needed it." He grinned. "I was slightly offended. She wanted to help, but it made me look at the life I've been dragging my family through since my wife died. The girls have never been allowed to decorate their rooms or even hang posters. Next month is their birthday, and they want a room they can decorate the way your girls have theirs. The plotting they're working on is about more than just my children wanting a real home. They want what you've given your girls."

She shook her head. "The human condition leaves us wanting what we don't have. I used to collect pictures from around the world and cover my walls with them. Selena once gave me a poster of Paris. I found one from Hawaii. My favorite was one that I had no clue where it was from, but I wanted to go there. The librarian gave it to me for helping her all year. When she asked if I wanted to go there, I was too embarrassed to tell her I had no idea where it was."

"Did you ever find out?"

"No. I thought it was better not knowing. I'd never be going, anyway, so it didn't matter." Her head tilted as a far-off look softened her face. "It's been over fifteen years since I've seen it, but it's still as clear as day. The gleaming white houses and pure blue roofs were nestled on cliffs along a beach with the most vibrant blue water. Nothing like the beaches we have here. There's no way it could be real."

"It's real. Santorini, Greece. What happened to your posters?"

"Santorini." She sighed. "My uncle tore them down." She continued putting the ingredients into the ice-cream maker, as though a young girl's dreams being shredded was no big deal. Then she stopped and looked at him. "Greece? Really? You've been there?"

"Yeah. A couple of times. My parents love everything Greek. Then I went once with Kari. It was a long time ago. Before we had kids." When they'd thought they still had a whole lifetime to explore the world. Since losing her, he'd avoided all the places where he had memories with her. Now, for the first time, he thought about their time together there and wanted to share it with his children. With Belle, too. That startled him.

When had the guilt slipped into something softer?

For the first time, sharing his past didn't hurt. "I could take you. It's even more incredible in real life." He watched her as ice and salt went into the barrel. "It's one of my favorite places after Tokyo. Have you ever traveled out of the country?"

She shook her head, not looking up.

"The United States alone is full of spectacular places, too. Have you seen the Grand Canyon or the giant redwoods? What's your favorite place you've been to?"

"I love the beach. People travel from all over to visit here."

"You're truly blessed to have this. It's an incredible place to live and raise kids. But if you grew up wanting to travel, where's the farthest you've gone?" He admired her, but he wanted to know more about her. She was the most closed-off person he'd ever met.

Maybe it was the challenge of discovery that had him interested in her as a woman in ways he hadn't felt since his wife. Belle was a mystery.

The only sound was the low humming of the small motor. She was so deep in concentration that her tongue stuck out.

A grin pulled on his mouth. Just sitting here on the porch with her ignoring him, a new kind of peace he'd never experienced settled around him. He wanted to belong here, with her.

He wasn't sure if she thought he had a place in her world. He needed to tread lightly.

"So," he persisted. The drive to know everything about her fired him up. "What's your favorite place to visit, other than your own beach? Granted, most people don't have a beach to call their own, but if you wanted to travel, you should. Then you get to come home to this. That's a pretty good life, Ms. De La Rosa."

With a heavy sigh, she turned from the ice-cream maker and faced the garden. "I don't have time to travel. There was never time. I told you I was sixteen when I had Cassie. I thought Jared was my ticket out of here, away from my uncle. But it was just like that old cliché. Out of the frying pan, into the fire."

"But you could have—"

She shook her head. Needing to avoid him, she checked on the ice cream. "She was born two days before the prom. Needless to say, I didn't go. I got my GED. There was a lot of normal growing-up stuff I skipped over. His family refused to acknowledge our marriage. We tried to make it on our own for a while. We lived all the way over the bridge in Foster after graduation. A few months later we were back on the ranch. There was no traveling. But," she rushed to say, "I wouldn't trade her for the world." Then she sighed. "Sometimes, I guess it feels like I did, but I don't regret it for a minute. She's better than all the places I never went combined."

He didn't like that he'd made her feel bad about herself. "Kids'll do that. Give you perspective. Mine kept me going when I didn't want to get out of bed in the morning."

"It's nice that you get along with your mother-in-law so well. It helps keep their mother with them."

He nodded, but he'd never thought about it like that. He knew they had helped each other through a huge loss, but Gina had helped his kids through their grief in ways he couldn't.

"She is a blessing. I'm not sure how well this would have worked out without her. She does most of the homeschooling. She homeschooled Kari until high school. Then Kari went into a magnet school for science and technology. Had her master's by the time she was nineteen. It took me a few more years." He grinned. "At twenty, I hadn't declared a major yet, but I had enough hours to be a junior. It took me twice as long to get my doctorate. She supported me every step of the way. I love what we were doing. I need my mother-in-law around because, at this rate, my kids will soon be too smart for me." He winked. "But I can't let them know that. They smell fear and doubt."

She chuckled at his joke. "I think you might be underselling yourselves a bit. I dreamed of going to college, but I would have had to leave the ranch. I certainly couldn't have afforded it and I didn't think I'd get a scholarship. Xavier and Damian went to the military."

He frowned. She said there hadn't been time to travel, but never leaving the ranch was unimaginable. Her cheeks went red as she busied herself checking the ice cream. He wanted to ask more, but she was already embarrassed. And here he was, bragging about Kari's education.

"If you had gone to school, what would you have studied?" He leaned forward, watching her every move.

"Agriculture. Husbandry. Before I had Cassie, my uncle and I hit every major city in Texas. He loved the attention. I have ribbons from the 4-H judging teams I was on, from horses to grasses. I learned a lot doing that. I also rode barrels and poles. Trained my own horses, too. I was looking to get a rodeo scholarship before…" She waved her hand and bit her lip. "I'm so grateful for everything I have. To think about what I don't have is a waste of time."

"You have a great life and have every reason to be proud of everything you've accomplished. I've seen the trophies and ribbons. Those were all before you were sixteen. Impressive."

"I was able to ride a little after she was born. Jared liked being on the rodeo circuit, too. The good ol' boy thing. I never got to see much of the places we went to."

Quinn was used to seeing her tall and bold, and he liked her that way. Not this woman who thought she wasn't good enough. "Belle. I'm sure you've learned by now that men who demean and insult the people in their lives are small-minded and lack self-esteem. It's all about their ego, not you. Don't be ashamed of your journey and how you had to accomplish this all on your own, either before you were a mother or after you became one. You didn't just survive—you thrived. And your girls are proof of that."

She checked the ice cream again. "Thank you."

He wanted to reach out and pull her against him, but he couldn't read her. Before he could act, she disappeared into the house and returned with a container of strawberries.

"Are those for the ice cream?"

She nodded and pulled a cutting board off the shelf above her head, then a knife.

"I haven't done much to help. Can I cut them?"

"Sure." Reaching up, she pulled out another board and knife. She rolled half of the strawberries over to him. Without another word, she began cutting hers into nice, neat slices.

"You know, I could cut them all. You should sit and relax."

"I'm not good at sitting. Doing stuff with my hands is how I relax."

As they cut in silence, he watched her hands slice and sort. Clean, efficient movements characterized everything she did.

Belle had fought for her way of life. Seeing the fierce way she loved the people in it had Quinn seeing new possibilities for his family. Even after being knocked down so many times, she was willing to try again.

He couldn't help but admire her. He finished cutting all his berries and then took a step closer to her. He put one hand on her arm. "Belle, I've been thinking—"

Ducking, she went around him and slid the slices into the ice cream. "We need to put the strawberries in. If we wait too long, we'll get ice crystals."

Was that her way of telling him to back off? He took her hand. "Belle. We're—"

"Mom! Is the ice cream ready?"

Chapter Sixteen

Belle jumped back. When had Quinn gotten so close to her? She started scooping the ice cream into a container. "It's all mixed. We need to leave it in the freezer for an hour."

"Oh, Mama! We don't have to. It's good enough as it is. Don't make us wait." Lucy flopped onto one of the rocking chairs with a dramatic flourish.

She laughed. "Waiting is good for you."

"What if it went into the freezer for thirty minutes instead of an hour?" Quinn grinned at her.

The rest of the gang agreed. "Yes! Thirty minutes. That's a good compromise." Hannah nodded and looked at Lucy. Her daughter agreed, even though Belle was pretty sure she didn't know what *compromise* meant.

"Here, Lucy. You and Jonah can put it in the freezer and set the timer." They ran to do their assigned job, and Belle finally sat, making sure to choose the rocker farthest from Quinn.

"Daddy. Did you tell Ms. Belle our other good news?" Hannah asked.

"That is not finalized, so no."

All three girls were sitting on the daybed with Frog across their legs. The Australian shepherd might be the best babysitter Belle had ever had.

"But Meg said you were staying," Cassie said.

"Staying?" Belle turned to him with questions in her eyes.

"Girls, I told you it was a family matter. We are not done discussing it. I haven't made up my mind yet, and I need to speak with Baba. You were not supposed to talk about it."

Their eyes met. "Belle, your face has gone pale. Not a good sign. This was not how I wanted to tell you about my plans."

"Sorry, Daddy. I'm just excited." Hannah dropped her head.

Meg finished off her sister's thoughts. "We love being on the horse-judging team. There's so much we could learn here. There's sailing. You love sailing and boating."

He rubbed the bridge of his nose. Then he looked at Belle.

"Is that what you were trying to tell me earlier?" It was easier to keep her distance when she knew he would be leaving soon, but what did it mean if he stayed?

As she massaged her temple, her fingertips touched the scar on the left side of her face. She didn't need a mirror to know what it looked like. It was burned into her brain.

It was the evidence that, no matter how strong she was, she couldn't always protect herself. The best way was to stay focused on her girls and the ranch. Quinn being in town for longer than a few months would not change her views on relationships.

She didn't want them, didn't need them.

"We love living on the ranch," Hannah said, and Meg nodded.

Cassie was between them, holding their hands. "Wouldn't that be great, Mom? They can help us with the chores and everything."

"No," she and Quinn said at the same time.

She took a deep breath. "Baby, that cabin was never meant for five people to live in. It's temporary."

Lucy and Jonah joined them. They climbed onto the porch swing. "What's temporary?"

"The cabin. We want y'all to move to our house and live with us. It's bigger," Cassie said.

"Wait. That is not what I said." Quinn's eyes darted to Belle. "I never said that."

The two youngest were all grins. "It's a great idea. They don't need to stay in the cabin. Jonah and I can share a room, right?"

Jonah nodded.

Lucy rambled on with their plans. "Cassie said the library could be turned into her room. If you get married, then y'all could share the big room. We have it all planned out." She grinned.

Quinn groaned and tilted his head back. Eyes closed, he looked to be praying.

Belle wasn't sure what to do. Man-to-man defense was not going to work with five kids against two tired, sleep-deprived adults.

"Stop. First, Mr. Quinn has not decided if they're staying in Port Del Mar, and this is a family discussion that we don't belong in."

"But we want to be family," Lucy said. Her head

tilted to the side in confusion. "Shouldn't we all talk about it?"

"We're friends." Belle squeezed in between Lucy and Jonah on the swing. Both looked as if they were about to cry. "Friends are a type of family, but not the type who talk about big life-changing decisions." She squeezed them to her sides, needing a way to change the subject. "Who's ready for fresh strawberry ice cream?"

That shifted the mood. Cassie and Lucy ran in to get the bowls as she retrieved the creamy dessert from the freezer.

"Can we watch a movie?" Lucy asked.

With the horde of little people happy in the family room, Belle handed Quinn the last bowl and sat in the rocker next to him.

"Belle, look at me."

Strands of hair wisped across her face in the breeze. Pushing them away, she bit her lip and turned to face him. The seriousness of his tone made her insides squirm. "What is it?"

He inhaled but kept his gaze locked with hers. "I do want to stay in Port Del Mar. I wasn't ready to talk to you because I wanted to make sure of my plans first. And that didn't include moving into your house."

He cleared his throat, then finally looked away. "I can rearrange my workload and make Port Del Mar my home base. I would still travel, but not as much or for as long. Mainly, I want to do this so we can explore a future. Belle, I think I lo—"

"Stop. We're friends. Don't…" The squirming insides tightened into hard knots. Unable to meet his gaze, she put aside her uneaten bowl of ice cream and stood. "I need to check the garden."

What she needed was space away from him. They were friends, that was all, and he was about to ruin it. What if they could have more?

No. No. No. She couldn't afford to go there. The scar on the side of her face throbbed as she fled to the garden. She was at the gate when she looked at her empty hands. No basket.

The gate was stuck. "You want to be difficult now? You think I need to talk to him?" she yelled at the garden gate. "There is nothing wrong with walking away from a fight." She rattled the latch. "Why are you being stubborn?"

"Are you talking to the gate? You have a habit of speaking to objects instead of people."

Her hands stilled, and she rested them on the gate. "They're easier to talk to."

"Because they don't talk back?"

The latch popped, and the gate swung open, causing her to stumble forward. Strong arms steadied her.

"You forgot your basket." Sure enough, it was hanging from his arm. "Belle, don't run. I want to give us time. We have something, and I don't want to walk away from it. Life is too short for us to ignore an opportunity to find happiness."

She turned to face him as he surrounded her in his warmth. As she looked up, their faces were so close that she could see each of his long eyelashes. Dropping her gaze, she traced the lines around his mouth.

Breathing became very difficult as he leaned in, torturing her with the slow progression. Finally, they touched, his lips gently nudging hers, asking for permission.

Pressing against him, she gave it. His arms pulled

her closer, and for that moment, she allowed him to become her whole world.

Stepping away would be the smart thing, but she was tired of fighting herself and just wanted to give in and absorb his warmth. It had been so long since anyone made her feel cherished. His hands rested at the base of her neck as his lips moved across her mouth.

"You're so beautiful and strong." His breath tickled her ear. He was so close but didn't kiss the sensitive skin. The muscles in his arm bunched and flexed under her hand.

His strength surrounded her. It would be easy to lose herself in him, but she had tried that before, and she'd lost herself. He was so different from Jared, but how much of the problems had been hers? She couldn't allow that to happen ever again.

For a moment more, she stayed there, captivated by him. Then, with a groan, she pushed away. He dropped his arms and let her go.

The basket he had carried out had fallen at her feet.

He shook his head, then picked it up. "I love you. I want more than friendship. We're more than friends already. I'm going to be around for a while. I'm making Port Del Mar our home."

"No." Betrayal made her want to cry. She never cried. She refused. "Why are you doing this? I told you I wasn't interested in that kind of relationship." She jabbed at the mark on her face. "I have this scar because I thought another man could save me."

How was she going to keep her distance if he was here? They could be friends if he was in another country, but next door? She wasn't strong enough.

"You don't need saving. I might not have a great

deal of experience with women, but I know what I felt from you when we kissed. That was not just friendship."

"So, I'm lonely. It doesn't mean anything." She stomped to the vines growing on the stakes and yanked off the beans, probably harder than they deserved. Without a word, he handed her the basket. She took it but made sure to glare at him.

He had agreed to be her friend, and now he wanted to ruin that. Her life was better without men complicating it.

"Belle. Please listen to me. This is why I didn't want to tell you like this. I wanted to get everything settled with the land and your mother. But the kids are so excited about...about having a real home and making us a family. They jumped ahead and... I'm sorry about that."

She stopped and stared at him. "Is that why you're doing this? To give your kids a mom? Mine need a father?" Acid was starting to burn in her gut.

"No. They have a mom. She's not here, but I won't ever let anyone replace her. She loved them so much." He looked over the walls of her vegetable garden. "For the longest time, I thought I'd never marry again. The guilt of her death was too much."

Belle gripped the basket tighter to her. "Quinn."

"I could have opted out of the job we were doing in El Salvador. If I had stayed home, she wouldn't have gone with me. There was an emergency, and we were trapped on the side of the road during a storm." He ran his fingers through his hair and studied the horizon as if all the answers were there. "She went into labor two months early. I couldn't get her to the medical care she needed. I couldn't."

"Was there a doctor?"

"No. I tried to drive us to the closest town. They had a midwife there. But there was a flood. She was so worried about Jonah. That's all she cared about. Making sure he was delivered safely."

She took a step toward him. "He was. As a mother, I'm sure that was all she was focused on."

He nodded, his breath low. "She had him in her arms when…" The silence was so heavy with his unsaid words.

"Oh, Quinn. You were alone with her?"

"Yeah. I didn't know what to do. All my education and none of it mattered. The most important person in my life and I couldn't help her. We were there for three more hours before the waters went down enough for someone to rescue us. She should have never been there."

"It seems to me she did what she wanted."

"Yeah. She was stubborn, hardheaded and determined. You're a lot like her. I seem to have a type." He grinned at her.

She jerked up. "What? We're nothing alike. She had more education than my whole family put together. She came from major money and a family who uses that wealth to save the world. My mother was stealing from us. Kari was tiny and petite and, if her mother and daughters are any indication, polite and soft-spoken. There is nothing soft about me."

"Those are all external qualities. At her core, you'd find a woman who fought fiercely for her family and her passions. She loved without holding back, and once you were hers, she never let you go." He cupped her face. "I love you, and I want to be yours."

"Oh, Quinn. I can't. It's too much. I can't love you

like that. I tried to be what other men wanted. It didn't work out. I'm not giving myself up again for a man."

With a sigh, she made her way to the house. Inside, Gina was sitting at the table. Belle didn't like the knowing smile on her face.

Did this woman really think she was good enough to step into her daughter's shoes? Not that her size tens would even come close to Kari's tiny feet.

"Oh, good. You're here. I was leaving you a note. I'm taking the kids into town. All of them. Jazmine's daughter is in the children's choir. It would be good for them to join her." She stood and went to the living room. "Everyone up. We're leaving."

"I can go with—" Quinn started to offer.

"Nope. Just me and the kids." She looked at them and lowered her voice. "You two need to talk. Especially if we're making Port Del Mar our new home." She winked, then ushered the kids out.

They stood there in silence for a moment.

"I guess we know where she stands." Quinn took her hand. "Come here. Let's sit and talk about this. You have valid fears based on your history, but that doesn't mean they should stop you from forming new relationships."

"We've already talked. Just go." Belle rolled her eyes. "Don't start analyzing me and my life choices." She pulled her hand out of his.

Being this close to him while he was telling her he loved her was too much. Her lungs wouldn't work. She needed her girls. She needed him to leave.

"I love how independent you are. I would never try to take that from you. I want a partner." He was close enough to take her hand again. "Can't you see a future with our families blended? This might be a little Neanderthal of me, but I can't deny the fact that I want to take care of you."

"I'll never give a man any control over me ever again. The ranch and my girls need all of me. I don't have time to make my hair perfect for someone else's pleasure or spend time worrying about what I eat because he thinks I need to be thinner. The clothes I wear and how I keep house should be no one's concern but mine." She stood and turned from him. She couldn't stop the stupid tears from streaming down her face as she relived all the pain her ex-husband and her uncle had put her through. "I've fought hard for my independence, and I can't go back to living for someone else's happiness."

She wanted to be a good role model for her daughters. She thought he understood her, understood that. Now he was changing everything.

He touched her back. Instead of pressing into him, she stepped away and wiped her face. "There's nothing to talk about. Please leave. I'm so sorry I can't be what you need."

"Belle." He reached for her again. "It's not about—"

"No." Stepping out of his reach, she went to her front door and opened it. If he stayed much longer, she'd cave—and she'd be left empty. More so than after her uncle or ex-husband.

With a heavy sigh, Quinn walked through the door. When he paused, she looked down. "Go. Please." If he stood there much longer, she'd be crying in front of him, and she'd never forgive herself for that. Or him.

Finally, he had moved far enough for her to close the door.

Pressing her back against it, she used all her weight

to keep herself from opening it and calling him. She waited to hear his boots on the porch.

Silence. He was still standing on the other side of the door.

"I know you're still there." His voice was low, but firm. "Belle, you need to know that there's nothing I'd change about you. Whatever they put you through, whatever they told you? It wasn't the truth. It was their insecurity. I wouldn't change a thing. You're perfect the way you are."

She covered her ears with her hands and waited for him to leave.

Chapter Seventeen

After warning Jazz she was going for a ride, Belle tacked up Little Lady. She needed more saddle time. Leaning over her neck, she let the mare run full out along the beach. She needed to cool the mare, so they went into the pastures and walked through the herd.

She had done this. Built the ranch up to solid ground. And she had done it without a man in her life. The sun was setting behind her.

She walked Little Lady to the grassy cliff near the rocky end of the coastline. Dismounting, she dropped the reins and let the horse graze as she sat on the edge, watching the tide roll into the shore below. This was her home. And, because of Quinn, she would be able to keep it.

God, I'm so torn. Have You sent Quinn into my life as a test, or as an answer to a request I was afraid to ask?

She struggled with trusting anyone and that included God. Talking with God, praising Him for all the good in her life, was easy. The weakest part of her faith, where she battled the most, was with turning everything over to Him. Trusting Him in all things was a fight she had a hard time letting go of.

After a lifetime of not trusting, how did she do it?

She twirled at the sound of leather behind her. Damian pulled up next to her and dismounted from a horse she didn't recognize. He did a little extra hop to maintain his balance, but even with that, she wouldn't have guessed he was missing half of his left leg.

His arm was another matter. He refused to wear a prosthesis. He'd been home for three years now and had seemed to adjust physically, but she had serious doubts about his mental and spiritual healing.

His faithful pair of Belgian Malinois followed him now as he made his way to her.

"Hey, Damian." Was this a private place of his? "Do you want me to leave?"

With a shake of his head, he dropped next to her. His dark hair needed a cut, and a heavy five o'clock shadow traced his hard jawline. He was probably the best-looking of the De La Rosa men—and that was saying something—but he was the most closed off. And again, that was some tough competition. The dogs settled in next to him and they all looked toward the ocean.

"If you want to come by the house, I can trim up your hair for you."

He ran his fingers through the silky waves, as if surprised by their length. "Okay."

"How is everything at the cabin? Do you need anything?"

"I'll leave a grocery list Monday. I'm good until then. Heard it all worked out with getting rid of your mother. How's the rest of the land deal going? Xavier came by and said it's looking good."

"It is."

He grunted, then turned to her. "So why are you out here, doing nothing but staring at the moon, when you aren't having problems?"

She laughed. "Am I that predictable?"

He shrugged. "What's up?"

Everything with Quinn was too complicated. "My mother doesn't care that we don't want her here. She just wanted money."

"That's how Frank got rid of her."

Startled, she turned to him. His full focus was on his dogs. "When? What for?"

"My mom wanted to keep you. She had worried about your mother's lifestyle. They gave her money for you to stay. Elijah butted heads with Frank, so it wasn't until later that Mother convinced him to pay for Elijah, too."

"Your parents paid for us?"

He made a face. "Not really. It was more like protecting you. Of course, after we lost Mom, everything changed. Your mother refused to take you back. She told Frank there was a no-return policy and left." He chuckled. "That made him mad. Of course, everything made him lose his temper. It was just a matter of degrees."

She nodded.

They fell into silence. Should finding out that her mother was paid to leave them trouble her? Letting the idea swirl in her brain didn't change anything. There was no connection to the woman who gave birth to her. But she did feel warmth that Mari had fought to keep her. She hadn't been unwanted.

Her traitorous brain did want to linger over Quinn, though. He'd changed everything about her.

What was wrong with her that she couldn't even talk about Quinn without wanting to cry? She didn't want another boyfriend or husband. She didn't.

"What's going on between you and Dr. Quinn?" Damian broke the peace of the waves.

"Did you just make a joke?"

He shrugged.

"Nothing."

"Liar. He's the reason you're hiding out here."

"Am not." She looked for something to throw at him for making her feel like a three-year-old.

"Did he tell you he liked you and now you're freaking out?"

She fell back on the grass, arms flung over her head. "I am predictable."

"I'm sure you can say the same about me."

"Yes. But you like being that way. No change. Keep it simple. No people."

"I like some people. I like you." This strong man sounded a bit like a toddler.

She grinned and nudged him. "Because I'm like your sister. You have to like me."

"Not true. Some would say you have to love your mom and dad. We're perfect examples of how that rule can—and should—be broken. You're my sister and I…" He took a deep breath.

She sat up. Was he going to say the word they all avoided?

"I care a great deal about you because I want to. You're an important person in my life. All us De La Rosas have relationship hang-ups. It didn't stop Xavier or Elijah."

"It wasn't a smooth road for either of them."

"No, but they did it, and so can you. With the right person. Quinn is that person."

She sat up. "Why Quinn?"

Pulling at the grass, Damian shrugged. "He likes you the way you are and doesn't want to change you. Frank and Jared were idiots. Don't let their voices be your truth."

"Those voices are very loud. Jared didn't start out that way."

"Yes, he did. He was a jerk at school. But you were a teenage girl in love, and he didn't spit his hatred at you then. Quinn treats everyone with respect all the time."

"He does."

"Belle, don't hide because of fear. A fear that those idiots planted in you. We should have stayed to protect you, but we had impossible situations, as well."

"Everyone keeps telling me how strong I am. That's not true. I wasn't strong enough then. What if I'm not now? I'm broken inside."

He shifted his leg. "You fought for us when no one else cared. When we didn't even care. You made this ranch a place we could come to and heal. You have so much to give. He's a man you can trust."

He paused, then looked at her, the bright moon reflected in his dark sea-green eyes. "You gave to the wrong people, but it doesn't mean you stop being you. You take care of people, animals, the land. It's what you do. He does, too. It's time you let someone love you."

Her throat narrowed. She opened her mouth to explain, but words didn't form. Damian wrapped his good arm around her and pulled her to him. The hard knot in her chest broke, and all the tears she had been holding back rushed through her. She sobbed.

The waves crashed beneath them as all the anger and sorrow poured out of her onto his shirt. She wasn't sure how long it took, but she was wrung dry. Leaning back, she patted the wet spot. "Sorry."

"Don't be. The strongest cry, Belle. It doesn't make you weak."

"You don't."

His mouth pulled at one corner. "Don't tell anyone, but yeah, I do."

The thought of him alone in his cabin, crying, broke her already cracked heart. She needed to make a point to visit him more often. Just because he said he liked being alone didn't mean he needed to be alone.

"You need to give Quinn a chance."

She shook her head. "I'm too broken."

His finger traced the scar on her temple. "Frank and Jared might have bruised you and left their mark, but they did not break you. Quinn's a good man. Give him a chance. He might deserve your love. I know you deserve to be loved."

"What about you? How are you going to find love locked away in that cabin of yours?"

"The world is better off if I stay in my cabin. It's not fear that keeps me there. It's that I'm the problem. No one wants or deserves me."

"Damian. That's not true. There are people out there who will see you and not what you lost. And you're amazing. Most of the time, I forget you're missing part of a leg. You could find the perfect woman for you if you did something other than talk to horses."

His laugh was rough and low. "Horses get me. It's not just my body that's broken. I'm pretty sure I'm incapable of loving. I'm too much like my father. My mother was the most loving woman, and she deserved better than what that man gave her."

"Damian, you're not—"

"No. It's not about physical appearance. I don't know how to connect. I'm broken on the inside in a way that can't be fixed. You have a chance with Quinn. Take it."

With the help of his dogs, he stood and went to his horse. "Belle, I want to see you happy. I've also started looking into Gabby's whereabouts. Our little sister is out there somewhere. I'm not going to interfere with her life. It's just to ensure she is safe and happy. That's why we sent her away. Xavier and Elijah are settled. You will be soon, if you're brave enough. If Gabby's life is good, that's all the peace I need."

He swung himself into the saddle and waited for her to mount. In silence, he followed her home, then took off to his single-room cabin in the woods, alone.

Her girls would grow up and have their own lives and families. Would she be as alone as Damian?

God, give me the wisdom to know Your truth. Remove the fear. The fear was a lie from the enemy.

What if she did open herself to Quinn and admitted she loved him? What would be the worst thing that could happen? He could discover she wasn't what he wanted and leave. But what if he stayed and they did fit together?

Fear was holding her back. Nothing else. That was not the example she wanted to set for her daughters. She loved Quinn, and he deserved to hear that from her.

Not wanting to waste another minute, she raced to the kitchen and grabbed the ice cream.

Just one knock on the cabin door and he answered

with a frown on his face. "Belle?" He stepped onto the porch and closed the door. "What's wrong?"

"I'm an idiot."

His eyebrows shot up.

"And a coward." She took a deep breath. "I love you."

For a minute, the world went quiet, and he stared at her, as though she had spoken a strange language. She held up the container of homemade strawberry ice cream. "You never got to eat yours. I brought you more. I thought you might want to start over. You know—tell me about your plans."

Maybe her arguments had been too good earlier. Maybe he'd realized he didn't really love her, after all. She took a step away.

"Oh, no, you don't. You don't get to walk away after you say you love me." He pulled her into his arms.

This time, instead of fighting it, she gave in.

"And you brought ice cream."

He took it from her and set it on the bench.

Leaning into his warmth, she sighed. His hand came up to cup the back of her head and his lips covered hers.

His love washed over her in a way that made her feel new.

This man loved her, and she loved him.

His lips went to her temple. "I'm afraid to let you out of my arms in case you slip into the night."

"No more fear. We both let fear rule our choices for too long. I'm stepping into a bold new future, full of love and hope. If you want to join me?" With a little space between them, she looked up to the most beautiful eyes. The love she saw there made her knees weak.

His large hand slipped into hers. "Every step of the

way. You aren't going to leave here and change your mind?"

She shook her head. "Nope. I'm yours forever if you want me. Are you sure you want to stay in Port Del Mar?"

"My favorite chair is here."

She laughed.

The door creaked open. Gina slid her arm out and grabbed the frozen container. "Carry on. I didn't want this to melt." And then she slipped into the house, the ice cream rescued from the Texas heat.

He laughed. "She approves."

"I'm not sure your family really understands they're going to be stuck in this small corner of the world."

His fingers tightened around hers, and he pressed his forehead to hers. "There are no rules that say we can't travel. Port Del Mar, the ranch, will be our home. But I want to show you the world, too."

She nodded. "I want to see it. With you by my side."

"The world just got brighter. I love you so much. Are you ready to hear that every day?"

"From you? Yes." She cupped his face and pressed her lips to his. He was hers and she was his.

Epilogue

It was a perfect April day in Xavier and Selena's backyard. The children stood in line as Buelita explained why they would be flowering the Easter Cross. It was a beautiful Easter tradition Quinn had never seen before.

Buelita stood before the four-foot wooden cross in front of a flower bed. She held up her flowers. "You each helped make flowers for the cross, and now you each have a real flower you picked from the garden. Christ died for us so we might have everlasting life with Him. The cross is a symbol of that sacrifice. Sometimes in our lives there's hopelessness, darkness and pain, but we celebrate the resurrection of Christ by covering the cross with colorful flowers that remind us of the new life He has given us. And the promise of hope."

The children all stared at her as she continued. "Flowering the cross is our way of giving thanks and reminding us of the love we have every day because of Him."

Everyone had a mix of roses, lilies and daisies, along with the small tissue flowers they had made. Each child in turn stood before the cross and placed their flowers with the others. Then, one by one, the adults did the same.

The reverence of the ceremony was not lost on anyone, even the smallest member of the De La Rosa family.

Quinn was surprised how moved he was by the simple action of placing his three flowers next to his children's. Once done, they all made a circle around the cross, now full of blooms, and Xavier led them in prayer.

Riff, Selena's father, held up three buckets. "Who's ready to hunt eggs?"

All the children yelled and cheered.

"This year, the moms are going to join in the fun," Xavier said as he lowered one of his triplets. More clapping.

Belle looked confused.

Jazz, playing along, held up her basket. "I'm ready."

"Belle, here's one for you." Selena winked at Quinn as she passed her cousin-in-law a wicker basket covered in blue and green ribbons.

Despite the cool breeze, sweat slipped down Quinn's spine. What if this was a mistake? She didn't like surprises. He knew he wanted to marry her. His girls had wanted him to make a grand gesture.

Everyone laughed as the kids ran around looking for the hidden treats. Cassie, the twins, Jazz and Selena were all trying to guide Belle to the large bright blue egg Quinn had placed high in a tree so the little ones wouldn't accidentally find it. But she was not cooperating.

So many things could go wrong. Cassie now stood under the tree that Belle had walked past several times. Belle had only one egg in her basket and it wasn't the right one. She wasn't even searching.

"Mom!" Cassie called her, then took off her shoe. Belle joined her, and together they looked at her foot.

Leaning on the tree, Cassie kept talking. She said something that made Belle look up.

She pointed, but Cassie shook her head.

Quinn moved closer. He wanted to get this over with. Was she not going to get the egg? He was going to grab it and give it to her.

"I can't reach it, Mom."

With a sigh, Belle stretched and plucked the egg from the fork in the tree. She handed it to Cassie.

Quinn was about to intervene when Jazz yelled from across the yard, "You saw it, you keep it. No giving your eggs away."

Laughing, Belle placed the egg in her basket with the other one. A few minutes later, Xavier sneaked up behind her and crushed a confetti egg on top of her head. Colorful dots rained over her, making her dark hair look festive.

From there, chaos broke out as people ran to either attack or to hide. Most of the time, they were doing both at the same time. Confetti was everywhere.

He pretended to see something on the ground, so that Jonah could sneak up on him and crack his *cascarones* over Quinn's head. He grabbed his son and tickled him.

Selena called everyone together to open their plastic eggs. As the family gathered at the long tables that had been pushed together, Belle was maneuvered to the end.

The triplets protested, wanting to crack more *cascarones* over people. They were each given one more and the adults leaned over so the toddlers could attack.

All smiles, and covered with flakes of yellow, blue, purple and pink, Belle took out her blue egg and shook it. Everyone stopped but pretended not to watch her. She looked at the table and frowned. Then she opened her egg.

She gasped at the little black velvet box.

Finally.

Quinn dropped to one knee at the edge of the table and took the box from her.

"Belle De La Rosa. In the past month, you have changed my life for the better. You've offered me a home and a family and a future. I love you and I want us to spend the rest of our lives loving each other and putting that love into action."

His throat went dry and all the words he had practiced caught in his lungs.

She covered her mouth and blinked at him.

"I love you more than there is water in the ocean and trees in the hills. Will you be my wife and join your family with mine?"

He held her gaze as he waited for permission to put his ring on her finger.

Tears moistened her lashes. "You're making me cry. I hate crying." She punched him in the shoulder.

"I'm sorry, sweetheart." With his thumb, he wiped away the tears on her cheeks. "I promise I'll do better if you say yes." He laughed. "I promise to fill your days with joy and to dance in the storms of life with you. I promise to love you with everything that is inside me. I promise to be the man that fills your life with laughter and to make your dreams become reality."

She covered her mouth. "Quinn."

"Is that a yes?"

"Yes. Yes. Oh, Quinn. Yes." She held her hand out and he slipped his diamond onto her finger. He picked her up and kissed her. Their families cheered and hollered. Soon they'd be one family.

"There's something else in the egg!" Cassie yelled.

Hannah handed her the egg. "You're not finished."

Belle took out the folded brochure. The gasp might have been deeper than the one for the ring as she stared at the travel destination. She looked up at him.

"Santorini, Greece?" She blinked as tears filled her beautiful eyes.

"Tell me when and it's our honeymoon. It was a backup to make sure you said yes."

She threw her arms around him and pressed her lips to his. He swung her up in his arms and pulled her close, never wanting to let her go.

"I'm so grateful you're strong enough to move orcas," she whispered in his ear.

He groaned. "I'm never going to live that one down, am I?"

She kissed his ear. "Nope."

"They mate for life, you know."

"That's good. Because once I give my heart, there are no takebacks. I'm yours forever." The promise in the words was solid and true.

"I'm good with forever." He bent closer until his lips hovered above hers. His Belle. "You're a gift I'll treasure every day. I promise." He sealed it with a kiss.

* * * * *

If you enjoyed this story,
look for the other books in the
Cowboys of Diamondback Ranch series:

Dear Reader,

Thank you for visiting and hanging out with the De La Rosa family. This is the third in the series and it has been a pleasure to learn their stories.

The coast of Texas is a very special place. One of the inspirations behind this story is Sea Turtle, Inc., in South Padre Island and their work to protect the natural habitats along the coastline.

In the 1980s, Kemp's ridley sea turtles had almost disappeared, but with joint efforts between Mexico and the US, the turtles are a success story and their numbers are on the rise. They are still endangered, but with the help they are receiving, there is hope.

I encourage you to find an organization that helps clean our oceans and beaches or a project that educates people about the animals that call the ocean and coastal lands home. We are stewards of this beautiful world.

I hope you enjoyed spending time in Port Del Mar with Belle and Quinn and their little family. Hope to see you soon.

You can follow me on Facebook at Jolene Navarro Author, on Instagram at jolenenavarro or on my website, JoleneNavarroWriter.com.

Jolene Navarro

The soup scalded Arden's tongue and gave him something to distract himself from the topsy-turvy way he was feeling. As he chugged down half a glass of milk, Rachel remarked how tired Ivan still seemed.

"*Jah*, he practically dozed off midsentence in his room."

"I'll have to wake him soon for his medication. And to check for a fever. They said to watch for that. A relapse of pneumonia can be even worse than the initial bout."

"You're going to need endurance, too."

"What?"

"You prayed I'd have endurance. You're going to need it, too," Arden explained. "There were a lot of nurses in the hospital, but here you're on your own."

"Don't you think I'm qualified to take care of him by myself?"

That wasn't what he'd meant at all. Arden was surprised by the plea for reassurance in Rachel's question. Usually, she seemed so confident. "I can't think of anyone better qualified to take care of him. But he's got a long road to recovery ahead, and you're going to need help so you don't wear yourself out."

"I told Hadassah I'd *wilkom* her help, but I don't think I can count on her. Joyce and Albert won't return from Canada for a couple more weeks, according to Ivan."

"In addition to Grace, there are others in the community who will be *hallich* to help."

"I don't know about that. I'm worried they'll stay away because of my presence. Maybe Ivan would have been better off without me here. Maybe my coming here was a mistake."

"*Neh.* It wasn't a mistake." Upon seeing the fragile vulnerability in Rachel's eyes, Arden's heart ballooned with compassion. "Trust me, the community will *kumme* to help."

"In that case, I'd better keep dessert and tea on hand," Rachel said, smiling once again.

"Does that mean we can't have a slice of that pie over there?"

"Of course it doesn't. And since Ivan has no appetite, you and I might as well have large pieces."

Supping with Rachel after a hard day's work, encouraging her and discussing Ivan's care as if he were…not a child, but *like* a child, felt… Well, it felt like how Arden always imagined it would feel if he had a family of his own. Which was probably why, half an hour later as he directed his horse toward home, Arden's stomach was full, but he couldn't shake the aching emptiness he felt inside.

She is going back, so I'd better not get too accustomed to her company, as pleasant as it's turning out to be.

Don't miss
The Amish Nurse's Suitor *by Carrie Lighte,*
available April 2020 wherever
Love Inspired books and ebooks are sold.

LoveInspired.com

LIEXP0320

SPECIAL EXCERPT FROM

LOVE INSPIRED SUSPENSE

INSPIRATIONAL ROMANCE

A murder that closely resembles a cold case from twenty years ago puts Brooklyn, New York, on edge. Can the K-9 Unit track down the killer or killers?

Read on for a sneak preview of
Copycat Killer *by Laura Scott,*
the first book in the exciting new
True Blue K-9 Unit: Brooklyn series,
available April 2020 from Love Inspired Suspense.

Willow Emery approached her brother and sister-in-law's two-story home in Brooklyn, New York, with a deep sense of foreboding. The white paint on the front door of the yellow-brick building was cracked and peeling, the windows covered with grime. She swallowed hard, hating that her three-year-old niece, Lucy, lived in such deplorable conditions.

Steeling her resolve, she straightened her shoulders. This time, she wouldn't be dissuaded so easily. Her older brother, Alex, and his wife, Debra, had to agree that Lucy deserved better.

Squeak. Squeak. The rusty gate moving in the breeze caused a chill to ripple through her. Why was it open? She hurried forward and her stomach knotted when she found the front door hanging ajar. The tiny hairs on the back of her neck lifted in alarm and a shiver ran down her spine.

Something was wrong. Very wrong.

Thunk. The loud sound startled her. Was that a door closing? Or something worse? Her heart pounded in her chest and her mouth went dry. Following her gut instincts, Willow quickly pushed the front door open and crossed the threshold. Bile rose in her throat as she strained to listen. "Alex? Lucy?"

There was no answer, only the echo of soft hiccuping sobs.

"Lucy!" Reaching the living room, she stumbled to an abrupt halt, her feet seemingly glued to the floor. Lucy was kneeling near her mother, crying. Alex and Debra were lying facedown, unmoving and not breathing, blood seeping out from beneath them.

Were those bullet holes between their shoulder blades? *No! Alex!* A wave of nausea had her placing a hand over her stomach.

Remembering the thud gave her pause. She glanced furtively over her shoulder toward the single bedroom on the main floor. The door was closed. What if the gunman was still here? Waiting? Hiding?

Don't miss
Copycat Killer *by Laura Scott,*
available April 2020 wherever
Love Inspired Suspense books and ebooks are sold.

LoveInspired.com

LISEXP0320